Float

Jacob Peyton

Published by Sleeping Possum Press, 2016.

FLOAT

First edition. December 13, 2016.

Written by Jacob Peyton.

Prologue

J ake Taylor and his brother Max knew they had gone too far out. They had decided it would be fun to take their little rowboat to the buoy; being 12-year-old twin boys, they had thought it was a great idea. Of course, that was before it became too hard to row back. Their father had often warned them about the tide. Now the boys were tired, and the sun was quickly sinking behind the small waves rolling across the bay.

Jake knew they were going to be in trouble when their father got home and found out what they'd done. That would be all she wrote for the rest of their summer. The only thing they'd have to look forward to was scraping barnacles and fixing pots, and whatever other chores their father threw at them.

"Well, at least we made it out to the buoy," Max said, trying to cheer up his brother. They both knew the beating that lay in store for them when their dad got home and found the boat gone. They wouldn't be able to sit down for a week. If they were lucky, it would end there. If not, he'd have them going out with him every morning on his fishing boat to keep them out of trouble.

Jake was afraid of having to spend the night on the water. He was also afraid of being pulled farther out. Growing up on the water, he'd learned to respect the bay and knew that they'd been a little too overconfident in their abilities. He also knew that at some point, their area of the bay spilled out into the ocean. What if they got pulled out to sea? He thought slowly, trying not to panic.

The boat rocked back and forth. They had tied it to the buoy so that the tide wouldn't carry them any further out, but he didn't trust the old rope they'd used to hold if the water got too rough.

The boys had left a note for their mother so she would know where they had gone, and now it looked like it would probably be used to find them. They both hoped they could catch the tide before it came to that.

As upbeat as Max was, even he didn't want to face their father's wrath. If Captain Taylor had to put his boat back out after he already came back in for the day, they would face it, no doubt about it. Add worrying their mother to that list and they wouldn't be sitting down comfortably for a month.

"At least we will have a story to tell," Max said suddenly, his smile returning.

"What do you mean?" Jake asked him, looking up from staring at the bottom of the boat. For a moment, he'd convinced himself that he could see water pooling at the bottom. Tapping his foot around he was happy that it was just his imagination playing tricks on him, together with their father they had put this rowboat together a couple of summers back if it started leaking, they were going to have a real problem on their hands.

His brother smiled wider. "Well, we'll be the only two kids in school that have stayed in the bay at night by themselves."

Jake shrugged, not understanding what Max was getting at,the only thing he wanted to do was put this entire nightmare behind him.

"Think about it. We can make up stories like old-time sailors used to. Ghosts, mermaids, sea monsters... anything we can think of." Max told him.

"We're tied to a buoy, faced with the very real possibility that we will spend the night out here and the only thing you can think of is what stories we're going to tell when we get back to school?" Jake asked him incredulously. It took all his willpower not to jump up in the boat as he said it, but the last thing either of them needed was to go overboard.

Jake shivered at the thought of it. He didn't like the idea of swimming after dark. Or even being out on the water after the sun went down boat or no boat, but like everything else in life, his brother seemed to take it all in stride.

Max just laughed, "Look, we have hours before the tide goes back in, so this way we've got something to do to pass the time." There it was. That look his brother made that somehow got Jake and the others to go along with even the stupidest of his ideas.

Like the time they all took turns shooting that hornet's nest with their BB guns, which stopped being fun the minute the hornets came out. When they'd told their parents what happened, Jake couldn't remember ever seeing his father laugh so hard in his life.

Even Jake couldn't argue the logic this time, though. They had hours until the tide turned and there wasn't anything else for them to do. The boat suddenly rocked as something hit it from underneath. "What was that?" Jake asked, his anxiety about being out here by themselves swiftly returning.

Max just shrugged. "I don't know; we didn't bump the buoy though." He said, perplexed. He looked over his side of the rowboat just to make sure. Then shrugged again. "Must've been nothing after all."

There was another bump, this time harder. The force of it rocked the boat violently. The boys looked at each other in shock as the third bump came. This one was so hard that it threw both boys out of their small wooden seats and onto the floor of the rowboat.

"What's going on?" Jake asked again, his voice shrill, close to tears.

"I don't know," Max said, his smile from earlier now completely gone. He now looked just as scared as Jake did.

The surrounding water wasn't choppy at all; the rowboat came back to the regular rhythmic rocking of the water. Whatever was doing this was coming from underneath the boat.

"Is it over?" Max wondered aloud. No sooner had he said it when the rowboat took another hit. This one came from directly beneath them, sending the rowboat up and over. In less time than they could scream, they went toppling out of the small, overturned boat and out into the water.

The boys hit the cold water and came up thrashing and gasping for breath as the saltwater stung their eyes. Their boat was capsized and there was no way they could flip it. Jake tried to rub his stinging eyes, but it was still hard to see. The only thing that stood out was the soft green glow of the buoy light as it gently rocked in the current.

"Jake!" He heard Max yell.

"I'm fine! Swim to the buoy!" He yelled back, unable to see his brother in the water. He couldn't see anything in the water. He heard a splashing sound that he took to mean his brother headed that way. Jake was closer to the buoy and swam for all he was worth.

Once he got there, he found the buoy was slippery, and it took some effort to pull himself onto it. After a few seconds of struggling, he pulled himself over the side of it. It wasn't very large, but there was enough room for him to lie on the side, gasping as he tried to catch his breath, holding on tightly to the mini tower as the buoy rocked in the waves.

He could almost have sworn that as he pulled himself up, something big brushed by him in the water, but he chalked it up to his imagination again.

"Stop it." He said aloud. No sense in scaring himself in an already out-of-control situation. From his vantage point on top of the buoy, he could see Max and their boat. The green flashing light on top of the buoy illuminated the darkness; casting everything in a dull, green glow.

Max, thrown further out, was thrashing in the water, from Jakes point of view it looked like his brother was trying to pull himself up onto the overturned boat. Jake, always the stronger swimmer, could only watch helplessly as Max seemed to fight the water, having to stop every few strokes to catch his breath.

Something didn't feel right to Jake, though. He saw nothing in the water that would have caused them to flip like that. It wasn't even windy enough for whitecaps on the waves. There weren't any sandbars this far out and if there was, their little rowboat surely wasn't large enough to run aground.

"Max, swim to the buoy! I'll pull you up!" Jake shouted. He wanted Max up there with him; something about the water was beginning to feel more sinister. Max turned to him and gave up trying to pull himself up on his boat.

Pushing off from the rowboat, Max swam towards the buoy.

Max suddenly started swimming faster and was getting closer to the buoy when, as Jake watched, he was pulled hard to the left. The water around Max churned as his brother briefly went under the water.

When Max popped back up, his face was white as a sheet as he started towards the buoy again. Clearly pushing himself much harder than before.

"Max, what happened?" Jake shouted, more afraid than he had ever been in his short life.

"Something hit me! There's something in the water!" His brother yelled, still sputtering water as he swam. Max's voice carried that slight tremble that Jake knew meant he was trying not to cry.

"Jake, it's something big!" Max shouted again.

Jake saw it first and the sight of it took his breath away, as he lay over the side of the buoy with his arm outstretched towards his brother. There it was a large fin rising behind Max, cutting through the still water like a torpedo. Jake shuddered as he felt himself go down a notch on the food chain and he relieved himself on the buoy. Too scared to even feel shame at the action.

He wanted to shout, to warn his brother, but the words wouldn't come.

Max, only a couple away feet from the buoy now, saw the look on Jake's face and looked behind him, then he screamed. It was a terrible scream, like a frightened animal.

Max looked at his brother and, in the green light, their eyes locked. Jake could only watch as a mouth full of razor-sharp teeth closed on his brother, pushing him the last little bit so Jake could grab his hand.

The green glow reflected in the shark's cold black eyes. His brother's screams were so loud that Jake's ears were ringing. He clutched his brother's hand and tried to hold on, but as the shark dove, he could only watch with wide-eyed terror as his brother was torn apart, forever pulled out of his grasp. Max didn't even have time to scream one last time before he went under one last time.

Even after the water stopped thrashing, Jake stared at the spot, waiting for either the shark or his brother to resurface. Neither one ever did.

When his father found him several hours later, he was still lying there on the side of the buoy, staring into the water, waiting for his brother to resurface.

Chapter 1

Henry was once again back behind a desk, fielding what seemed like an endless amount of customer service calls. Just like he'd done every day for the last seven years, making him wonder if there had even been a point in him getting a degree. Not that a bachelor's in history was very marketable unless he wanted to teach, which was the last thing he ever wanted to do. He couldn't imagine a worse fate than being stuck in a classroom with a bunch of kids who just wanted to use and abuse an adult as a verbal punching bag.

Though, anything would be better than having to deal with customers calling him as if he could somehow fix all their problems, only to curse him when he couldn't. Which most times he couldn't, it wasn't like he could go back in time and get these people to make better financial decisions.

If he were honest with himself, he would have walked away from this job years ago, but if he up and quit, Cheryl would probably leave him. These days when he thought about it, he couldn't help but wonder if that might not be such a bad thing with the way their marriage had been going of late.

The only reason he had this job in the first place was because his oldest friend, Tim, had stuck his neck out for him years ago. Henry couldn't return the favor by just walking out on him. No matter how much he wanted to.

Thoughts of Cheryl came rushing back into his mind. These days he couldn't decide which was worse: going to work or coming home. The phone started ringing again, cutting off his train of thought. He chucked a pen across his office in retaliation.

The sudden violent movement caused him to laugh. Is this how nervous breakdowns start? He wondered, and not for the first time.

Look at me throwing things around like a toddler having a tantrum. What he needed now was something to shake up his life right at the foundations. If not, he didn't think he and Cheryl were going to last.

Hell, he honestly didn't know if he even cared anymore.

That's when he remembered something Tim had talked about earlier in the week. He let the phone go to the answering service, and he walked out of his office and headed over to Tim's. He walked boldly across the gaggle of cubicles and bee-lined over to Tim's office door, daring any of those other paper pushers to say anything to him.

God, I hate my job. Henry thought again, angrily. Wondering why he'd let Tim talk him into it all those years ago. Even though the simple answer was money, and Henry's lack of it.

Not to mention if he left, he'd probably just end up in another customer service role somewhere else. Somewhere that wouldn't put up with his moodiness.

He stopped outside of the door to admire the large brass nameplate that adorned the door to Tim's office: Tim Flannery. In big letters. He was sure that Tim's ego got a kick out of that every time he went in. After all, he was one of the few people in the office to have a brass nameplate, especially one that big. It practically took up the whole door. It wouldn't suprise Henry in the leat if it he found out Tim bought it himself.

People on the street could probably see it, he thought with a chuckle, giving the door a complementary knock and paused in the doorway a moment before walking in.

Tim looked up, all smiles, as usual. Henry had known him long enough, though, to know it was part of the act. Part of what made his oldest friend so good at his job.

"Henry, what's up? Is it time for lunch already?" He asked, looking at Henry and then at his watch.

"No, it's not quite time for lunch yet. I wanted to ask you whether you were serious about that thing you had mentioned earlier this week?" Henry asked, being as vague as possible. Knowing that Tim would drag it out and make him ask, since he was the one who shot it down in the first place.

"What about trying out that new Thai place?" Tim chuckled, "You sure you want to eat something that spicy? It's hotter than Hell out there today."

Henry realized he was going to have to be the one to say it. "The charter boat thing you were talking about."

Tim beamed, a shit-eating grin spreading across his face. "Oh, I thought you said that was a stupid idea."

Henry fidgeted and looked away. "Yeah, well, I've been thinking about it... and I don't know, it sounds fun." He said, his hands gesturing nervously the whole time. He hated having to admit he was wrong, especially to Tim who was a giant man child, and the only friend he'd kept in touch with after college.

Tim leaned back on his desk and crossed his arms in front of his chest. "It would be good to get out of the city for a while. Besides, four days on the Chesapeake bay on a party yacht might just be what everyone needs around here."

"It's on the bay?" Henry asked.

"Well, it goes from the bay, out into the Atlantic, and back," Tim said, deep in thought. "Besides, the yacht has a hot tub on it, so we won't be swimming or anything in the bay. And we'll all be drunk so it won't matter what body of water we're on."

They both laughed at that.

Henry couldn't wait to tell Cheryl about the trip. She was always complaining about how they never went anywhere anymore. Well, this would show her and, even better, the company would foot the bill.

Ever since Tim had attended some seminar series on synergy in the workplace, he had become obsessed with the company's synergy. He had been going on and on, talking to all the section heads and managers and their respective partners about letting the office go on a getaway. Henry didn't understand how getting everyone together to get plastered, do trust falls, and make poor decisions were supposed to improve sales, but apparently Tim did, and if he could get to use it to get Cheryl off his back and maybe blow off some steam, then it was a win-win situation as far as he was concerned.

He was so excited by the prospects that he even let Tim convince him to try that Thai place for lunch. Which he regretted as soon as he walked in and smelled the spices wafting through the restaurant. The only thing Tim loved more than gimmicky self-help seminars was searching out the most authentic restaurants.

The last time had been a Mexican place where the food had caused Henry to spend his weekend with his face in the toilet. If he hadn't been so hungry, he probably wouldn't have been able to eat his food now. He had ordered Pad Thai on instinct since he had it at a couple of chain restaurants. This version was so spicy he was pretty sure his tongue might actually be blistering.

He really couldn't wait until Tim got on an Italian or French food kick. Or maybe, if he was really lucky, it would be food trucks and greasy burgers. Things his wife hadn't let in the house in years, ever since she jumped on the organic food trend.

Henry cared less about farm-to-table than he did about what his neighbors did in their spare time; another topic his wife found endlessly fascinating. The things she found interesting threatened to push him deeper into the bottle. Yeah, a cruise is exactly what they needed.

He knew she was going to be in one of her moods as soon as he walked through the door. When he saw that the television was off, he knew it was going to be a bad one. She was sitting there, silent, on the couch. The look of scorn that had become so familiar these days had long ago replaced the cheerful face he'd fallen in love with.

"Well, look who's home late!" Cheryl snapped at him as he sat his briefcase down. Her red wine sloshed in the glass. Great, here we go again. He thought miserably.

Henry just sighed. He knew that no matter what he said, it would only make her angrier, and that was the last thing he wanted. It was better to just let her blow up. She would later calm down and they would both pretend it never happened.

When did this become my life? Henry couldn't help but think as he grabbed the bottle of wine and took a seat in his faded green recliner, and waited for the continuing onslaught of his wife's screaming.

As she called him every bad thing she could think of, he just stared at her, trying to find some hint of the woman he had fallen in love with. Her blonde hair was still there, as were her blue eyes. They had some wrinkles around them now, and that hunger for life that had once dominated them was long gone. She was still in there, but it was somewhere deep down. Had they both changed so much over the years?

By the time she finished screaming, he had polished off the rest of the bottle. As she walked out of the room, he yelled out to her.

"Hey! Tim invited us on a cruise, if you're interested." He heard her stop in the hall. "I mean, it's nothing fancy, just a work thing, but I figured you might like it." He knew it probably startled her. The look on her face was probably priceless. The fact that they hadn't taken a trip in years was something they fought about often, that and the fact that life hadn't turned out the way they'd planned. The other reasons weren't something he wanted to think about...at least not without another bottle of wine.

Chapter 2

Captain Jake Taylor calmly piloted his fishing boat back into the bay. It had been a good haul all in all. He'd be able to pay the crew a bonus and get some repairs done to his boat during winter when his commercial fishing business came to a halt for several months.

Looking ahead at the calm skies, he decided it would be a good time to let the men have some time off. The season was ending, and they had certainly earned it. Jake had been pushing them hard lately. He always did this time of year...too many terrible memories. He supposed he should call his father and get it over with, just to check in with him and make sure that he was alright. Maybe he could even avoid having to see him in person at all.

Besides, they had been getting extra in the nets the last couple of runs, and maybe driving out to see his father wouldn't be the worst thing he could do with his own free time, he knew that no matter what he decided he would end up regretting it later. As they pulled into the marina, he ran his cracked and calloused hand through his sandy blond beard. It had been too long since he had last seen him; he thought again.

Damn, come to think of it, they hadn't seen each other since mom died, and that had been just the two of them standing around with a smattering of friends and family, barely saying a word to each other or anyone else for that matter. As far as Jake was concerned, there was nothing left to say. Not anymore. He just really couldn't believe that it had been that long. Since then, it had been phone calls here and there and loose talks about visits that Jake could always push off by using work as an excuse.

The men finished unloading the boat quickly as the wholesalers were already on the docks, ready to buy up as much of the catch as they could. Something about all the restaurants wanting their seafood fresh off the boat now. Whatever, at least it saved him the trouble of having to store any of it. It was shaping up to be a good year for Taylor Fishing LLC, with his one-boat armada pulling out as much as legally possible from the Atlantic.

"Have a good leave, Captain!" Several of the men hollered back at him as they grabbed their gear and made their way off onto the marina and heading to their vehicles, happy to have some time off. He waved to them, silently wishing them the best and wondering how many of them would be back the next time he set out.

Deckhands always seemed to come and go, especially once they got some money in their pockets, but it seemed to be worse lately and not just on his boat. Something to ponder on another day. Today he had to deal with his father now that he had set his mind to it.

He ran his hands along the rails of his boat. Small enough to maneuver through the bay and big enough to fish commercially in the Atlantic: it was all his. Right down to the name: *The Angry Lady*. Most people assumed his ship was named after a lover, but the truth was he named it after his mother, who had been furious that he had taken up his father's profession instead of going to college like she had wanted him to.

The truth, however, is that she would have been happy if he had just done anything else. She had gone to her grave, terrified of losing another son out in the water. Damn, not even sundown, and he was already thinking about Max. He needed a stiffer drink before he went down that road.

After all, he liked to think that they had to be kind of proud. His father had never owned a fishing boat. Instead, he had spent his life working in other captain's crews until his body wasn't able to anymore. It was a hard life and fishermen rarely retired without injuries to show for it.

Jake was coming up on forty and already had to fight to get out of bed in the morning. If he was honest with himself, he probably only had another 15 years of this ahead of him. And that was being generous. But, with a boat of his own, he could just sit in the chair and order the others around. Hell, he should have stopped being so hands-on with everything ages ago if he'd wanted to.

He had put off leaving as long as he could, double and triple-checking everything on the boat. He went into his quarters and grabbed his duffle bag, quickly swapping out his big rubber boots for soft, well-worn sneakers. A sigh of relief escaped him upon taking off the boots. Compared to them, the sneakers were like walking around barefoot. With one last look at The Angry Lady, he blew her a kiss and stepped off onto the dock.

His truck was right where he had left it a week ago, before this last run, too ugly to steal, just another rusty Dodge pickup sitting outside the marina. Unlike The Angry Lady, which was kept in pristine condition, the only compliment a person could give about his truck was that it still ran. The thirty-year-old Dodge was mostly rust and duct tape, which suited Jake just fine. He had never been much into vehicles that ran on land.

As long as it ran and passed inspection, he would drive it until the wheels fell off.

From the sounds the truck made when he turned the key, he knew it would soon be time for him to look at the used car lots. He pulled off onto the highway and made his way to his father's house.

After his mom had passed, Jake's father had sold their house and moved into a small rancher right in town. The move had caused more arguments between him and Jake, but he knew his father was right in the decision. The house held too many bad memories for them both, and the smaller house was easier for his father to manage.

It was already dark when he pulled into his father's driveway and parked behind the old maroon sedan that was his father's pride and joy. The kitchen light was still on, which was good. He thought of calling over on the way and had decided against it.

Mostly, it would have been awkward and unnecessary. There was no way the old man would be asleep tonight. Jake didn't even know if he was going to be able to sleep tonight. Not with the memories of his brother swirling around in his head.

He walked up to the door and was about to knock when it opened. "Didn't anyone ever tell you to turn your damned lights off when you pull into someone's driveway? You lit up the entire house, you know that." His father told him. Which was a friendly greeting coming from the old man.

The word "old" ran through his head as he looked at his father. John Taylor had not aged gracefully: his skin was wrinkled and leathery from years spent working out on the sea and his back bent from years of abuse. His beard, which he'd always kept neat, was now long and untrimmed, but looking closely, there was still a familiar fire in his eyes. Enough to let him know his father was still a long way from kicking the bucket.

"Well, you just gonna stand outside all day, or do you want to come in and have a drink?" His father bellowed.

Jake simply nodded and followed him inside. They went into the kitchen. His father's house was cluttered with junk. No, that was putting it nicely; the man was close to being a hoarder. Old newspapers lay stacked up in corners and filled the shelves, but Jake knew why he kept the ones he did. He knew that if he opened them up, he would find an article somewhere in there with a very specific topic. A topic that tonight of all nights he wanted to avoid like the plague.

He didn't want to go there right now and instead accepted his father's offer of hard liquor. Not even pausing when John poured them two glasses of bourbon. Far from the top shelf stuff, but it would do just fine; he took two slugs out of the glass, relishing the burn as it tore down his throat.

After the glasses were empty, his father retrieved two cold beers from the fridge. It was an old ritual and, with a sigh, he knew his father had something he wanted to talk about. After he set the drinks in front of them, his father cleared his throat.

"I suppose you know what today is?" He asked rhetorically. They both knew neither of them could forget, no matter how much Jake wished they could.

"It's been a long time, Dad," Jake said at last. Not knowing exactly where his father was going with this, he used to add, and it's time to move on, but he knew all too well that it would do no good. No matter what, his father was determined to never move on.

"Your brother should be here with us." His father said, changing from his usual routine this time of year.

Jake looked up. "I know, Dad, I know. But there's no changing the past."

"I don't want to change the past. I want the damned shark that ate my son!" His father all but yelled.

Jake was at a loss for words, wondering where all this was coming from. And why on tonight of all nights?

"It's probably already dead by now," Jake said, cradling his beer, letting its frigid chill penetrate his palms and calm his nerves. "You know those things don't live forever, and it's been what, thirty years, give or take?"

His father shook his head, his long gray beard sweeping the table in front of him. "I'm telling you, it's not and what's more, I think it's heading this way."

Jake laughed, regretting it as soon as he did. "How would you know that, Dad? You haven't been out on the water in years."

His father opened his arms, gesturing at his house. "It's here. It's all around us. Every attack and sighting of it. All reporting the same thing, an 11 foot Bull Shark attacks on people all along the rivers and coastlines of the Eastern Seaboard, from here to Florida. So how's that for an old man who hasn't dipped a toe in the water for years?" His father all but roared the last part.

Jake gasped. He knew his dad kept articles about shark attacks, but had never thought there was a method to his madness. Saying nothing else, Jake made his decision and hoped it was the right one. Standing up, he went over to the counter and put on a pot of coffee.

They had a long night of planning ahead of them and they would need more than cheap liquor and cold beer to get through it.

Chapter 3

E ver since he told her about the trip, Cheryl had hardly spoken a word to him, although compared to recent months, that wasn't a bad thing. She had been happy while they were packing, but perhaps the thought of bringing their troubles on a boat full of people was getting to her. It was sure getting to him. Henry was already trying to come up with excuses for why they shouldn't go as he loaded the card.

But before he knew it, he was behind the wheel of their ten-year-old sedan, heading to the marina.

There were a fair amount of people already on the dock when they arrived. Henry had never been on anything larger than a canoe in his entire life, so the sight of such a massive yacht took his breath away. Cheryl's hand found its way into his as they both stood there, staring at it.

Yes, this is exactly what they needed. Maybe it would be a pleasant trip after all. He told himself, feeling pretty optimistic about the entire thing.

Tim stood in front of the yacht, checking in everyone as they climbed aboard.

Henry barely recognized him. He was wearing a Hawaiian shirt, swim trunks, and flip-flops, and to top it all off, a costume captain's hat sat on top of his bald head. He looked like some kind of Gilligan's island reject; a far cry from the suit and tie that Henry had seen him every day since they had graduated college.

Had it been that long since they'd all hung out? He wondered, trying to remember when he and Cheryl had stopped going out and became the married couple that were in bed by nine every night.

"Welcome, friends and coworkers once you're on board this vessel there is only one rule... and that is that the party doesn't stop until we reach the shore!" Tim shouted the last part, getting a happy roar in response from the gathered crowd. Without further ado, the passengers boarded the yacht.

One of the ship's stewards led Cheryl and him onto the ship and down its twisting hallways and into their room. Tim had told them they'd been given the second largest since Henry was his good friend and a senior man in the office, as far as he was concerned. Henry took that with a grain of salt. He had long suspected that Tim knew there was trouble at home and just had the common courtesy not to bring it up. Henry never talked about it to anyone, but had always suspected that it showed on his face somehow. He never had much of a poker face.

Cheryl gasped as they walked inside.

Henry just stopped and stared, slack-jawed, for a second. Their room was absolutely beautiful. The bed was enormous, with nightstands and armoires that he was pretty sure were walnut. Henry hadn't been expecting that. He had thought they were going to be in bunks or hammocks or something.

Tim really had gone all out for this trip. And why not? They deserved it wasn't like the company was losing money.

"Is that a California King?" Cheryl asked him as she put her belongings down on the comfortably carpeted floor.

Henry whistled. "Sure looks like it." He jumped on the bed first, letting out an "oomph" as he landed. He didn't know how it was possible, but the bed was even more comfortable than it looked.

"Henry! Look, we even have our very own bathroom." Cheryl called over to him.

He turned over to look and sure enough, there it was. It looked like something out of those resort shows she liked to watch all the time. Tim had gone all out for this trip, that was for sure. Without thinking about it, he stood and walked in. Henry snaked out his right hand and playfully grabbed Cheryl's butt; a gesture that he hadn't done spontaneously since they were much younger.

She looked at him, shocked, and then giggled. The sound of her laughter was something that he had sorely missed. He ran a hand through her long blonde hair and pulled her into a kiss. His other hand wrapped around her waist and pulled her closer to him. Using his foot, he closed the door to the bathroom.

They made love twice in the shower. By the time they were done the second time, both of them were out of breath: they hadn't done something like that in quite a while. Especially at the spur of the moment. Most of their sexual activities were as planned out as the rest of their lives these days. It had been refreshing to say the least, Henry thought, a smile plastered across his face.

They lay together on the massive bed. Their nakedness barely covered by the soft, plush, white robes they had found in the bathroom.

"You know what I need right now?" Cheryl asked him, snuggling closer.

"What?" He asked, staring up at the ceiling and thinking of simpler times.

"A cigarette." She said with a laugh.

Henry laughed too. She hadn't smoked since their late twenties, but when she had, both of them would always share an after-sex cigarette. Henry had never been much of a smoker, but some things were hard to pass up back then. He thought, unable to look away from her.

Just then, there was a loud knock on their door.

"Room service!" Tim's voice came from the other side. "Hey, guys, come on up to the main deck. We are having a Luau." He called again from the other side of the door.

"Sure thing, man," Henry called out, just to get him to leave.

They listened as Tim retreated down the hall.

"I guess we need to be going then," Henry said, even though a part of him was sad that the moment was ending: time for them to get back to the real world. At least the vacation was working out the way he had hoped. As they got dressed, he could no longer feel what was there only moments ago, and from the look on Cheryl's face, neither could she.

After dressing, they left their room and made their way up the stairs. They were still in the bay so it wasn't so bad, but already Henry could feel faint nausea every time the ship rocked. He could only imagine what it would be like once they hit the ocean. It was something he didn't want to think about.

At the top of the stairs, they were greeted by a petite stewardess, who immediately put a necklace of plastic flowers around their necks. Looking around, the party was in full swing. Some of the accountants were in the hot tub with either their wives or girlfriends, with glasses of punch in their hands. Henry could smell the punch bowl from where they stood. It had to be loaded with enough rum to make a pirate gag.

He filled up two glasses for him and Cheryl. She wrinkled her nose when she took it, but drank it all the same. Tim was like a wild man; running around, talking to people, and making sure everyone's drinks were topped off. He and Cheryl took a seat overlooking the water and watched it pass by in mostly silence: neither one of them hardly spoke a word to each other. As he drank, more and more Henry wondered if they could ever recapture that moment from earlier or if it was gone forever.

Chapter 4

Jake Taylor couldn't believe his eyes. For years, he had thought that his father's obsession with shark attacks had stemmed from his inability to let go of the past. Never in his wildest dreams would he have guessed that his father was tracking the same shark that had killed Max this whole time.

He wondered how long his father had been tracking the shark. The old man had boards filled with tidal charts paired with attacks going back years. Attacks that went up and down the eastern seaboard from Florida to New York. The shark didn't seem to mind the occasional detour into a bay or river, either. The more he looked at everything, the more he realized his father was right. This shark had to be stopped.

This shark had taken too many lives, and if they did nothing and his father was right, then it was about to take a lot more.

It had taken him more than a couple of cups of coffee to realize that there was a method to the old man's madness, he thought, bleary-eyed. Organized was not the word he'd used for his father's evidence, which lay in boxes scattered all around the house.

They had spent the rest of the night going over all of his father's research and damn it if he wasn't beat. The sun had long since risen and his father had gone to bed a couple of hours ago. But Jake just couldn't seem to stop reading and re-reading all the articles his father had collected. Especially the more recent ones. The more he looked at them, the more it sank in that this was all real and his father wasn't just a delusional old man.

Jake was on his second pot of coffee and was just starting to feel tired. He felt like complete shit, but could not look away from the articles and news clippings. Some were not labeled as shark attacks, but as drownings. That's what his father had looked for after a while.

"If there isn't a body and no witnesses, then there's no attack." His father had told him solemnly sometime around two in the morning.

The pattern was there, though. On a large map in the living room, his father had the shark's migration pattern labeled out. Every year it went down the coast into Florida waters and then returned up the Eastern Seaboard and into the Chesapeake Bay before heading farther north; every year for over twenty years. Pins all up and down the board show deaths that his father thought were suspicious enough to be the shark.

"And perhaps longer than that, but I only started from Max's attack. At first, it was a hard thing to swallow, you know, a shark attack, but when I saw more and more, and then the drownings along its hunting grounds. It was all too much of a coincidence to not be the same shark."

Jake couldn't imagine how someone, a marine biologist or even the Coast Guard, hadn't noticed the pattern. But in a way, he supposed, they wouldn't look at these and think it was the same shark for each. Instead, they would look for multiple sharks. Hell, he still barely believed it. If his father's research was to be believed, one lone shark was responsible for a lot of deaths. Including his brothers'.

But what was he going to do about it? Search the waters from here to Florida? That was ridiculous.

No, wait. He ran his rough hands through his goatee and rubbed his sore eyes. His father had said something before he had gone to bed; something that had kicked off this late-night session.

It was coming back.

That's what he had said and one way or another, they had to stop it for good.

Jumping out of his chair, he went back to the map into the living room. It was coming back. Following the lines his father had painstakingly plotted, he sucked in his breath. If the old man was right, in a few days the damned thing would be right back where it had murdered his brother all those years ago, and the images that had haunted his nightmares since that night filled his mind.

I'm too tired for this, he thought miserably, and made his way to the couch. The sun was already up outside and he could already hear his father moving around in his room down the hall. And why would he not? John Taylor had been a fisherman all his life and Jake knew damn well those habits die hard. He had barely hit the couch before sleep took him under.

When he woke up again, he saw it was now well into the afternoon. His father was in his tattered, old armchair sipping brandy, and from the redness of his cheeks, it probably wasn't his first glass. Jake's head was pounding; an aftershock from the alcohol and caffeine that had kept him fueled throughout the night.

"Well, what have you decided?" His father asked him.

Jake yawned and ran a hand through his hair. There was no sense in pretending he didn't know what his father was talking about.

What was he going to do? He wasn't even that sure yet. Looking back at the map, he made his mind up. Each one of those dots was a life.

"I'm going fishing." He said finally.

His father sighed in relief. "Good. Guess we need to get the gear on the boat then. Back your piece of a shit truck up to the garage."

Jake arched an eyebrow, but knew better than to argue. Now that he agreed to help him, his father was back to acting normal: another crotchety old man who was mad at the entire world. Jake sighed. He knew there was nothing to gain by arguing with him at this point.

Outside, the truck sputtered a few times before finally turning over. He knew soon he would turn the key and it wouldn't turn over at all. His father was right. It was a piece of shit. After this was over, he'd have to look for a new vehicle.

His father had the garage door up and was already throwing stuff into the back. Jake whistled when he saw some of it: dive knives, spear guns, a shotgun, a rifle, and even an honest-to-God harpoon gun. Well, at least now he knew what his father spent his social security check on besides bourbon, brandy, and beer.

"I already made us some sandwiches. Let me go grab my pistols and the crossbow." His father told him excitedly as he turned to head back inside. He stopped just inside the door. "Oh, grab that green box; it's full of ammunition and has some dynamite I bought off a road crew some years back." He left Jake standing in the garage, gaping after him. Jake made a mental note not to grab the green box and instead tucked it further into the garage. The last thing he needed was for his father to accidentally blow them up.

He hesitated for a moment, wondering if they wouldn't need it, but finally tucked it away out of sight. Although, when he thought of that night, the thing had seemed huge to him. Maybe dynamite wouldn't hurt. Ever since he'd fished deep water, he'd been catching sharks usually by accident. And while a bull shark was big, it wasn't exactly massive. Part of him felt like this was a lot of overkill for one little shark. The other part of him agreed with his father.

The attack was a long time ago, and I was just a kid at the time; he reminded himself. Besides, this was all just the culmination of his father's hate for the shark... and his regret at losing Max.

He sighed and decided, tucking the green box carefully into the truck so it wouldn't roll around. They probably wouldn't end up using it anyway, but having it aboard would make his father happy. And the longer he could keep the peace between them, the better.

They ate their sandwiches in silence as they made their way to the marina. Perhaps his father knew deep down that Jake hadn't wanted him to come along. His father was too old to be helpful on the boat, but he knew that there was no way that he could keep him away. Looking at him now, Jake knew why: this was his last chance to go out and get it.

If he was honest with himself, he'd have agreed that they both needed this and there was no chance of them getting in trouble over this; as long as they left the shark in the water. He took the last bite of his sandwich and got out of the truck, ready to finally put the past behind him and get the closure that he and his father deserved.

Luckily for them, there was nobody out on the docks when they arrived. It took them less than twenty minutes to unload the truck and get it all stashed away inside the ship.

John may not have stood on a ship in years, but he quickly re-found his footing and quickly went to work unmooring the ship from the dock. With one last look at the marina, Jake and John Taylor put out after their shark.

The Angry Lady was officially on the hunt.

Chapter 5

Mike Yves and Harold Johnson were night fishing, a summer pastime that they had done since they were kids. Some things come and go, but for them, this would never change. As long as they could move about and had strength enough to cast a line, they would continue to fish together.

They were even in the same boat; a small, wooden, single-engine fishing boat. It had been repaired and repainted over the years, but at its core, it was the same boat they'd taken out when they were much younger men. Back when small boats were often built by the same people that used them.

But, a lot had changed over the years, including their small southeastern fishing community. While it was still southeastern, it was no longer tiny and the people who lived there certainly didn't have time to build their little boats, instead they bought up cheap little plastic ones that didn't last half as long as Mike and Harolds had.

At least they could still go fishing, Mike thought to himself, happy that out on the water, he couldn't hear the sounds of the interstate.

"Catch anything yet?" Harold asked, his face dimly outlined by his lighter as he sparked up yet another cigarette. Followed by a hacking cough, Mike politely turned away. Harold had started smoking the summer after they'd built the boat and hadn't stopped since. It looked like it might be starting to catch up with him. But that wasn't fishing conversation, that was drinking talk, and they weren't ready for that yet.

Mike couldn't help but think that Harold was smoking more than he used to, but he couldn't help but wonder what he would be like if it was his wife who had died. Which also wasn't a fishing conversation, Mike reminded himself.

Mike reeled in his line, noticing it felt a little light. "A couple of bites, but nothing huge." When he got his line in, he swore out loud, "Something keeps taking my bait, though."

Harold laughed as Mike cut up more of the peeler crabs they were using for bait. Mike had wanted to use squid because he felt like he caught more when fishing with squid, but Harold already had the peelers. Mike couldn't stand the peelers. He always had the damnedest time getting them on the hook and, more often than not, ended up pricking himself with it in the attempt.

Whether or not they caught anything, at least it was a pleasant night, Mike mused. After all, fishing for them wasn't all about the catch. Most of the time, it was just about getting out of the house. Something that seemed to be more important with every passing year.

The moon was large and bright in the sky, making it easy to see over the water without light, and the stars shone brightly overhead. There was even a small, cool breeze that kept the humidity at bay. The perfect night for fishing. Now all they needed was to catch some fish. They had already been out for two hours with nothing to show for it.

On the boat, they had two coolers; one for drinks and snacks and one for fish. One was empty, and the other was slowly getting there. With a sigh, Mike cast his line back into the water. It went right where he wanted it and gave a satisfying plunk as it hit the water and dragged the line and bait down below the surface of the waves.

"I think that's the spot," Mike said hopefully.

Harold chuckled again. "You've been saying that every time you've cast your line tonight. Yet, you've got nothing to show for it."

"Yeah, well, this time I have a great feeling," Mike told him, running his hands over his now bald head, a nervous gesture leftover from when he had hair.

"Yeah, a real good feeling," He said again, this time with a little more conviction in his voice. Harold simply laughed again without turning around.

Just like before, Mike felt several small bites. He relaxed his grip on the pole, knowing that he would reel it in to put more bait on it in no time.

Oh well, he thought. There was nothing he could do about it. Suddenly, there was a hard pull on his line and he almost dropped the pole. He pulled it tight and started laughing. Mike laughed again when he saw the look of disbelief on Harold's face.

Whatever he had on the other end was big. He was pulling, but he could barely get it to budge. If this thing was half as big as its pull, then they would need a bigger cooler, he thought with a laugh.

Oh, man, please don't let me be hung up on something in the water. That would be embarrassing. Glancing over at Harold, he knew that if that was the case, his friend would never let him live it down. Besides, that would be impossible; they were in deep water and his sinker wasn't heavy enough to drag down to the bottom.

Another hard pull almost took the pole right out of his hands. The only way he kept it was by propping his feet up against the side of the boat and using his legs to push himself back. The line suddenly went slack. For a moment, Mike feared it had broken. As he reeled, he realized that whatever was on the other end had turned towards the boat.

Probably an eel or a skate; the thought comforted him, since they gave a pretty good fight. Although, if that's what it was, the cooler would stay empty since neither man ate eels or skates.

Only one way to find out. He gave another hard pull on the line. Whatever was on the other end changed directions, shooting away from the boat. The ripples were just visible in the moonlight. This time, the pull was so hard; the pole flew out of his hands and splashed into the water. The sudden release of tension caused the boat to rock violently. Harold was laughing so hard he had to hold his sides.

Mike could feel his face turn red from embarrassment. "Yeah, well, at least I hooked something." He muttered, wishing he had brought a spare pole.

There was a splash several feet away from them and then a ripple as something charged towards the boat, the pole bouncing through the water behind it.

"What the hell?" Harold said, before whatever it was, struck the boat hard enough to make them drop their poles and grab the sides of the boat.

When it stopped shaking, they both just looked at each other; wide-eyed and scared. In all their years fishing out here, nothing had ever violently charged their small boat.

"Let's get out of here!" Harold hollered, tossing his pole into the bottom of the boat.

Mike didn't have to be told twice. He scrambled over to the engine and started pulling the pull string and waiting for the old engine to turn over. "Come on baby, come on." He muttered.

He sighed in relief when it made a loud chugging sound. He revved the throttle while Harold hastily pulled up the anchor.

"It's up!"

Mike heard him shout. He revved the throttle and sent the small boat jolting forward.

Something rammed the boat from the side, sending them off course. Both men could stay in by gripping the sides of the boat hard, but just barely. Harold sat on the floor of the boat. His pole and the coolers went overboard. Mike couldn't help but notice how scared his friend looked, and he realized then that he probably looked the same way.

Before he could get them going again, something struck them hard right in the center of the boat. Whatever it was, had come up from under them, throwing the front high in the air.

He heard Harold scream as he was thrown from the boat. Mike hadn't even thought to scream as the cold water rushed up to greet them.

He bobbed for a moment and then tried to swim towards the boat, but he was out of breath. Mike hadn't been in the best of shape for quite some time, so his swim was a slow one. He saw Harold, who was just a little way away from him. They both made their way to the still upright boat. Hopefully, they could climb in without flipping it.

From his left, he suddenly heard Harold scream. "Something's got me!"

Mike swam faster as he watched Harold bob in the water. The saltwater made it hard to see straight, and his eyes burned. When he had finally cleared them, he could no longer see any sign of Harold. In the moonlight, he could make out that the water was darker over where he had been.

He swam harder, gasping and sputtering. It was getting harder for him to breathe, and his chest was starting to feel tight.

Something big swam underneath him; he felt its large mass rub against the bottom of his boots and the water suddenly became several degrees colder. For the first time in his life, he was afraid of the water.

He struggled as he tried to climb up the boat. His hands found their way to the rim of the boat. Suddenly he felt a sharp, tearing pain in his leg. Whatever was pulling him down, causing the boat to rock. Whatever it was, he could feel its teeth cutting into him. Unable to keep his grip, he felt his fingers slide uselessly down the sides of it as he was dragged into the water.

The shark pulled Mike deeper into the churning water. He kept trying to reach out towards it. But, the boat got further and further away.

"Help!" He screamed. "Somebody!"

But there was no one around to hear him. The teeth went away for a moment. Mike, however, knew it wasn't over.

A fin rose and sliced through the water at him. Already starting to black out from blood loss, the last thing Harold saw were the dead black eyes and many rows of cruel teeth that dragged him down into the depths.

Chapter 6

"We need more chum!" John Taylor yelled to his son. Jake could barely hear him from where he was sitting in his captain's chair. Already regretting his decision to go on this voyage. He'd been so caught up in his father's theories and the alcohol certainly hadn't helped either.

Now he felt like they were on a wild goose chase. Jake couldn't help but wonder if this had all been a mistake. When he'd been looking at the articles and news reports, it seemed so tangible, but now he wondered if that was just because he'd wanted to believe.

If the shark was still out there, then he had a tangible enemy. One he could fight, defeat, and finally put an end to the nightmares that plagued his dreams.

Now, less than a day later, he was having regrets. They had already killed two sharks, but both were four-foot bull sharks. There was no way either of them had anything to do with his brother's death or anyone else's. That fact hadn't stopped his father, however, from dragging them on board and killing them with the excuse being that he was making the waters safer. Jake would have thrown them back on principle. He took pride in his work and they weren't in the ocean yet. Catching a killer shark was one thing, getting caught poaching sharks was another. Last thing he wanted to do was lose his ship and his livelihood.

Jake would not let that monster, or the search for it ruin his life.

Not again.

That was when Jake realized that, for his father, it was very unlikely that they would ever find the right shark. He watched as the old man grabbed more chum all by himself and dumped it over the side. Then started putting more bait on his large hooks. He threw them off the side where they would be pulled along beside the boat.

And what would happen if they found the right shark?

An image of it flew through Jake's head of those emotionless, black eyes, causing him to tighten his grip on the wheel. What would his father have left if he got his revenge? Jake didn't like any of the answers that flitted through his head.

His father hooked nothing else, but that didn't keep him from walking around the deck and rechecking all the lines like a madman. His pale, old skin already showed splotches of red from sunburn. If he noticed it, he said nothing about the pain.

A call came out over the radio. Jake wasn't paying attention until he heard the Coast Guard come across asking if anybody had seen two missing fishermen on a small craft. He quickly replied, asking where they were last seen. When they replied, he checked his charts and saw that it wasn't far from their current position and, even worse, it followed his father's plotted path of the shark's hunting grounds.

He ran down to the deck. "Dad, pull the lines!" He shouted.

His father looked at him with a wild look in his eye. "Why would I pull the lines? Any minute we could get it, just be patient."

Jake shook his head, "No, you don't understand, two fishermen just went missing south of here. They were on a small boat, night fishing. And it's right here on your path." He told him, pointing to the map of attacks they had taken from his father's living room.

His father's eyes widened with understanding and both of them began hastily pulling the lines back in. They wasted no time turning the boat to the south. Jake quickly changed their course. He hoped they found those two men alive. There was a lot that could go wrong night fishing in a small boat. They could have simply capsized and been swept away by a powerful undertow.

It sounded a little too like his own experience with the shark in a way that Jake couldn't shake. Something about this call gave him a feeling in his gut that their monster was behind it.

His father peered out over the deck with a pair of old binoculars, constantly surveying the water for any signs of the fishermen or the shark as they got closer to their last known location.

Jake had to admit that the old man looked better than he had in a long time. He looked like he finally got some life back into him. His father raised a hand, letting him know he spotted something. Jake deftly maneuvered The Angry Lady in that direction. Keeping a careful eye on his fish finder and depth reader in case he saw anything big swim by.

He dropped anchor and walked out onto the deck. His father was waiting for him and the old man looked almost giddy with excitement.

"What do you see?" He asked him.

"Look for yourself," his father replied, pointing to the side of the deck out into the water.

At first, Jake didn't realize what he was looking at. Then he saw it. A large object flipped over in the water. He realized it was a well-kept little wooden boat. With what looked like a small Yamaha prop on the back. Nothing fancy, but for a couple of weekend fishermen it would get the job done.

"What kind of shark attacks a boat?" He asked his father. Still squinting at it.

His father snorted. "The kind we're hunting. Mark my words, son, this shark has a taste for man and it's not afraid to make a bold attack. It's figured out what we've known all along. We're apex predators, but only on land get us in the water and we're done. Me and you, we can get it with hooks and bullets safe on a big boat with something sturdy under our feet. But in the water, we're sitting ducks. Never in a million years would we out swim it, and it can get us from any direction before we even realize it's coming."

He spat out into the water before continuing. "This monster knows that a small boat like that is nothing more than a floating lunch box. All it's got to do is tip it over."

Jake thought about it, remembering the night his brother had died. Hadn't it done the same to their boat? Had it already been hunting people when they crossed paths with it? Or were they first? He didn't want to think about it.

"I told you it had an M.O." His father said, clasping his hand on his shoulder, "You need to stop thinking about it as just another fish." He told him, turning Jake and looking him right in the eye. "The thing we're hunting is a monster. Never forget it."

With that, Jake went back up to the control room and radioed back to the Coast Guard, letting them know he had come into contact with a flipped-over boat. He read the numbers on the side. It matched the description of the boat used by the two missing fishermen, just like he feared it would.

They continued to circle the site, but there was no sign of them. Jake wished he had a drink, but knew he had to keep his head in the game. If the shark was smart enough to do this, he didn't have any room for error. If his father was right, according to his notes, this thing was just getting started.

He continued down his father's path, following the migration pattern his father had carefully made over the years. This attack happened just last night. They were closing in.

The old man had gone down below deck to get some rest while he could. The weather responder suddenly beeped, letting him know that a large storm front was moving up from the south. If they kept their path, they were going to head straight into it. It wouldn't be the first storm Jake Taylor had gone through, but with everything else that was going on, he couldn't help but think of it as some type of ill omen of things to come.

Part of him wanted to just anchor the ship and wait for the storm to pass. But he knew if he did, his father would give him grief for as long as he lived, especially when they were so close. He went down onto the deck and made sure everything was battened down. The last thing they needed was hooks and gear flying around in the oncoming gale. With a sigh, he set his course, matching it directly with the shark's hunting grounds. Hopefully, they wouldn't lose it in the storm.

The Weather Station came back across the channel, letting people in the water know that the storm was now being categorized as a tropical storm and for all vessels to either return or try to avoid it, especially smaller ones.

Jake wasn't worried, but he knew he would be in for a long night. He went down below deck and turned on the coffeemaker. He'd need all the caffeine he could get to see him through. With a cup in hand, he went back to the wheel and set a course directly into the heart of the storm.

Chapter 7

Henry was drunk, too drunk. After what had happened with him and Cheryl while aboard the yacht, he had been so happy that he had thought drinking with Tim was a good idea. Henry couldn't match Tim drink for drink back when they were still in their twenties and he damn sure couldn't do it now. However, that didn't stop Tim from constantly topping off his drink and proposing a toast every ten minutes. It was Henry's fault; he supposed. It was the first time in years that they'd all drunk together, and it looked like his friend planned to make the most of it.

Shit, he thought, trying to keep his legs under him as he navigated the narrow confines of the yacht. What a stupid vacation idea, he thought as he fell into the wall for the fifth time in his attempt to stay upright. The entire world seemed to spin around him. Now Cheryl was going to be mad at him again. She hated it when he drank too much. It was one reason he'd stopped going out with Tim.

Henry lurched again as the yacht seemed to jolt under his feet. Was he that drunk, or was the water getting rougher?

His thoughts quickly went back to Cheryl. Surely she would understand that it had been Tim's idea and Tim had gotten the company to pay for it after all. So, of course, he had to drink with him. He hoped Cheryl would at least understand that and not get too mad. Finally, he saw the door to his room and flopped onto his bed. Groggily, he sat up long enough to take off his shoes, then remembered he'd been wearing flip-flops that were already off.

He laughed as his hands touched his bare feet. How long has it been since I've been this drunk? Henry wondered and flopped back down. He sank into the bed and hoped he didn't puke. If he puked, Cheryl would never let him forget it.

He'd already gotten sick twice up on the deck and didn't think he had anything left on his stomach. Half because of the alcohol and half because of the choppy water. At least he hadn't puked on her, a miracle from the way his stomach felt.

Take that romance, but she seemed to enjoy herself, and they weren't fighting, which was a victory in his book.

The captain of the yacht had given him some pills that helped to ease his nausea somewhat. And since then, he and the rest of Tim's friends had spent the rest of the voyage getting completely and utterly wasted. Leave it to good ole Tim to make sure this place was well stocked. Cheryl had partied with them some at first, but had seemed to grow bored with it. Their first night together, however, had gone back to being just as good as when they were younger.

He must have passed out at some point. It had to be early in the morning. Henry woke up suddenly as he fell to the floor. His head was still spinning. Henry didn't understand at first what was happening. Then the yacht pitched again, sending him sprawling back onto the floor.

What in the world is going on? He wondered, getting up and walking into the hallway. Keeping his hands flat against the walls to stay balanced.

Looking around, he didn't see anyone in the hallways and no one popped out of their bedrooms. He put a hand to his head, trying not to be sick. Henry had to squat down for a minute to try to decompress. Everything around him felt like it was spinning.

Everyone must still be in the galley, he realized as the yacht took another hard hit which threw him into the wall. This time, he slid back down onto the floor.

He grasped at the railings with his hands, trying to pull himself back up. For the second time tonight, Henry spewed. This time it was all in the hallway and ran across his bare feet. He moved away from it quickly, afraid that the rocking of the boat would toss him into it. Then he would end up being sick yet again.

The hallway finally gave way to the stairs, which went up to the upper deck. He still couldn't hear the others, which bothered him. His knuckles white on the rails, Henry took a deep breath, trying to stay calm and keep his legs under him at the same time. Carefully, he took the steps one at a time. The last thing he wanted was to fall down the stairs.

Gently does it, he thought, putting one foot in front of the other.

Another violent toss and his legs shot from under him. The only thing that kept him from sliding down the stairs was his grip on the railings. He winced in pain as his right knee bounced painfully off of the stairs.

Gasping in pain, he pulled himself up. Henry felt his panic rising as he finally cleared the stairs. The upper deck was empty. So was the galley. What he noticed, however, was the dark sky. Lightning crashed in the distance and illuminated the massive swells as they crashed into the yacht, spewing dark water across the deck. Looking at the storm, Henry realized that until this moment, he had never truly been afraid. Watching the storm, he felt utterly powerless, and that terrified him in a way he'd never felt before.

He stumbled, at last realizing where everyone must be, and headed that way, stumbling up yet another small flight of stairs. Henry tried to listen for the others, but outside he couldn't hear anything over the sound of the storm. Luckily, as he climbed the last step, it turned out he was right. They were all huddled together in the control room.

The captain, a stern-looking man with a name tag that said Taggert, stood with his hands gripped tight around the controls. He was concentrating on the water in front of him. Lights blinked and flashed all over the wheelhouse in a way that Henry doubted was good. Beads of sweat ran freely down the side of the Captain's face, and the man made a pointed effort not to look any of them in the eye.

Whatever was going on, Henry knew it couldn't be good. More than anything, he wished that he'd drank more. He didn't want to sink scared and sober.

He dimly realized that everyone was up here, even the other crew members. Each one of them was even wearing life vests. They had vacant faraway looks in their eyes as though, like him, they couldn't believe what was going on. Most of the other passengers were in various states of sobriety.

Cheryl saw Henry and threw her arms around him. He gripped her tight in return. She had tears in her eyes and Henry tried his best to put on a brave face, but he was way out of his element here and they both knew it. He knew nothing about the water and as far as he knew, neither did she. Before this, the biggest emergency they'd encountered as a couple was a flat tire. He'd much rather be changing a tire on the side of 95 right now than be on a yacht in a storm.

Out of the corner of his eyes, he saw Tim in the corner cradling a bottle of scotch.His friend was drunkenly bawling his eyes out; another reminder that shit had indeed hit the fan.

The Captain looked back at them, his face a mix of emotions as he stared out at the storm. He muttered something about the weather coming upon them faster than he'd expected and then uttered a curse as yet another gigantic wave smacked into the side of the yacht and sent passengers and crew alike stumbling around the cabin.

Looking around at his crew as they struggled to find their feet, the Captain seemed to solemnly decide something muttering another curse before staring off into the distance. Henry's mind raced as he struggled to keep up with all the events going on around him.

"Prepare the life rafts." the Captain commanded them, his voice completely deadpan as yet another massive way crashed into the yacht, rocking it. Something down in the ship's guts made a chunky grinding sound that Henry doubted was good. Smoke billowed from the back of the yacht. Henry could make out the inky black clouds even in the dark..

The yacht was no longer moving. Henry gulped and his heart thumped wildly in his chest as he realized they were officially dead in the water. He'd seen enough movies in his lifetime to know that wasn't a good thing.

It dawned on Henry that the older man was trying not to panic. He wanted to keep everyone calm for as long as possible. Nobody moved when the yacht seemed to even out for a minute. Henry realized he had never talked to the Captain before this and he and Cheryl had missed the safety seminar during their little afternoon delight. Now he wished they hadn't. Then they'd know what they were supposed to be doing right now.

The Captain grabbed his radio. "Mayday-mayday. This is the Skylark....."

There was a little more after that, but before he could ask what it meant the first mate escorted Henry and the rest of the passengers out. He wished he knew the man's name. He thought, in a situation like this you should know everyone's name, but if they all got out of this alive, he figured he'd have plenty of time to learn it.

Another swell crashed across the bow and swept over the ship, sending furniture and anything not bolted down to the deck straight over the side and into the sea. All other thoughts, except for staying safe, fled from Henry's mind. The first mate was explaining to them that the raft would go overboard and then self inflate. Tim and others cried out anew at the thought of going into the water. Henry didn't blame them.

Henry and Cheryl just clung to each other. As far as he was concerned, there wasn't anything else to do. He'd always been a realist and knew that they were all going to get into the water whether they liked it or not. At least getting on the raft would give them a better chance for survival.

He pulled her closer, hoping against all odds that they would make it out of this. He realized that some stewards and other crew members were having breakdowns as well. Another clear sign that shit had indeed hit the fan. At least the first mate seemed to keep it together, which was good because they needed someone to lead them out of this.

Henry became increasingly numb to the whole situation. The whole thing was just feeling too surreal. It felt like he was watching it all from someone else's perspective.

The whipping of the wind and crashing of the thunder made it hard to hear the first mate as he handed out life jackets and emergency beacons to everyone. These had little lights on them and clipped onto the life jackets. That way, if they got separated, they'd be able to see each other.

Henry remembered that much from watching some documentary and knew they were so the Coast Guard could find survivors from the air. He also remembered that in a lot of cases, it was used to help retrieve the bodies. But he had the good sense not to say that part out loud.

The little blinking box in his hand didn't make him feel any better. In fact, he didn't like the fact that this was all that stood between him being found or him being lost at sea forever. Buckling his life vest, he quickly attached the little box to it, hoping that it wouldn't have to be used.

"Do you think we're going to be okay?" Cheryl asked him as he helped her put her vest on. She was trembling, but he didn't know if that was from nerves or the rain. He figured it was probably a bit of both and wondered when he was going to feel the same way.

"I honestly don't know..." He told her. "But I won't let anything happen to you." He added, hoping he sounded braver than he felt.

She gave him a little smile in return, instead of the usual snarky comment. He gulped. If Cheryl wasn't calling him out in the moment, then they were definitely in trouble.

Together, they joined the other passengers in a single file as they jumped off the side of the yacht. Someone grabbed his elbow. He turned, surprised to see the first mate there.

"I want you to stay back and help me get everyone off!" The man shouted to him to be heard over the storm, though Henry still had trouble hearing him over the wind.

Henry was about to argue, but looking around, he realized he was the only other person not on the verge of having a complete breakdown. A few of them were clearly going into shock. Still, being partially buzzed was probably the only thing keeping him from feeling the same way.

"Okay!" He yelled back, giving the other man a thumbs up just in case he hadn't been able to hear him. The first mate returned the gesture and Henry followed him to the front of the line.

Before they jumped, the first mate instructed the three crew members who would go over the side first to swim to each other before activating the raft. That way, they could help the passengers get aboard.

Next, he instructed the people in the water not to fight the waves and tire themselves out. Just thinking about it made Henry shudder. He had never been an overly strong swimmer. He'd also never had to swim like his life depended on it, either.

One by one, the crew went over. Henry couldn't bring himself to look as they hit the water. The swells were massive, and he was dreading going over the side. Next came the guests, many of whom he barely recognized. Below them, something in the ship groaned and the first mate shouted for people to hurry as the engine seemed to seize and the yacht listed, no longer pushing its way through the waves. Now it just shook as it tossed and turned in the storm.

For a minute, he thought he would have to push Tim over. He just stood at the side and wailed. Henry had never seen the big man so upset. An enormous wave kept him from having to do it. The force of it hitting the side of the ship sent Tim overboard. He screamed as he went over, but the sound was cut short as he hit the water.

Cheryl was the last one to go over. She grabbed his hand as she neared the edge. Henry knew that there was nothing he could say that would make the situation better. Before she jumped, she threw her arms around him and kissed him before turning around and jumping off the ship. He hoped it wouldn't be the last time he kissed his wife.

He and the first mate nodded to each other. He took one last deep breath, steeled himself, and took the plunge. There was a moment of weightlessness as he sailed through the air and then a splash as cold seawater soaked into the very fiber of his being.

The rough water pushed and pulled him every which way as he fought his way to the surface. If it wasn't for the life jacket he probably would have drowned.

His eyes burned as the salt water rushed into them. Henry looked around and realized that he couldn't see any of the others. He rose and fell with the churning water. Lightning crackled overhead, but all he saw in every direction was the roiling dark water.

As the sea raged around him, Henry found himself completely alone.

Chapter 8

When Henry woke up, his whole body was stiff and achy. The only thing he wanted to do was stand up and stretch, but that was impossible without going in the water. He'd floated for a minute before the First Mate had grabbed him and pointed towards the raft. By the time they could get aboard, he'd all but passed out from exhaustion.

At least the storm was over, but even the gentle rocking of the raft did little to calm his nerves. Overhead, he could feel the sun beaming down on them. Already some of the other people on the raft were showing the beginning signs of sunburn. Henry had been smart enough to put some sunblock on before going up to the deck the other day. But it was only a matter of time before he fully sweated it off. His skin was already feeling hot and achy.

As he looked around at the others, someone moved beside him.

"Morning," Cheryl mumbled to him as she rubbed the sleep out of her eyes.

He didn't reply, just slid his hand in hers and took in the scenery. Not that there was much of it. All around them, as far as the eye could see, was open ocean. Greenish-blue sea water churned in every direction. The yacht was gone. He remembered the sounds it had made before he and Tyson jumped.

Had it sunk? Once he was in the water, he wasn't even able to see the yacht anymore.

If he hadn't drunk so much the other night, maybe he'd have been able to ask someone why they were jumping overboard. He thought, mentally kicking himself. This was exactly why he'd stopped drinking with Tim to begin with.

Speaking of drinking, he also needed to piss, bad. He saw some others going off the sides of the raft and swallowed his pride. Deciding that he'd wait until he absolutely couldn't hold it or until dark, whichever came first.

Henry saw the man who had helped him earlier sitting off to the side. The First Mate had a forlorn look on his face as he dug around a small black bag at his feet. He caught Henry looking at it.

"It's a GPS, like the one on your life vest, but this one is like the ones used by airplanes when they go down." He told him and then cleared his throat. "It's so the Coast Guard can find us faster." He croaked, his voice already cracked by their lack of fresh water. "There's also a little hand radio in here, but I don't want to waste the battery until we see a ship."

Henry nodded and turned at the sound of splashing. He saw some of the other survivors drinking the salty seawater, voraciously using their hands to shovel it down their mouths to cool their throats. Cheryl moved to follow suit, and he grabbed her arm. She looked up at him questioningly.

"Don't drink that. It will just make you thirstier." He told her.

All those survival shows were finally coming in handy. However, unless they washed up on a deserted island filled with fish and goats, he had a feeling that the salt-water fact was the only thing that was going to help him.

The first mate nodded to him. "Smart. I told them that too before you woke up." He said, looking at some of the people still trying to choke down the brackish water.

The hours dragged on with the sun forever beating down on them. Whatever their natural color was before getting on the raft, they were all now several shades of red. Tim was the worst. Already, Henry could see the blisters rising on his bald dome. At first, they had talked amongst themselves, but as the day wore on, it became harder and harder to talk with dry mouths.

It was even worse for those among them who drank the seawater. They had gotten a wild look in their eyes; something between panic and madness. Henry remembered how on one of those shows the guide had said that if people kept drinking saltwater, they'd hallucinate from dehydration. Just like how people in the deserts saw mirages.

He had whispered to Cheryl to monitor them, waiting for the moment that they behaved erratically, or worse, put them all in more danger than they were already in. They didn't have to wait long. One man, a small guy with a pencil neck and receding hairline, was the first. Henry was pretty sure he was from the accounting department.

"What are we doing?!" He croaked, rocking the raft as he tried to sit up. "There's all that water out there and we are just sitting here!"

Henry held Cheryl back as the others tried to stop him, as the man tried to stand. Some part of him knew what was about to happen and knew they couldn't help. Tim and the first mate tried to pull the man in, but he kicked and punched until the raft started rocking violently, and then came the sound of a loud splash.

"Dear God!" Cheryl cried, holding tighter onto Henry.

Pencil neck didn't even try to climb back in. They could hear him swim for a little while. Then his splashing stopped. What struck Henry the most was how the man in the water never called out for help. In some part of his dehydrated brain, he must have known he was about to drown, but he didn't shout out. He just accepted it.

Experts say that drowning is the most peaceful way to die, he thought numbly, hoping they wouldn't witness anyone else make the same choice.

Unfortunately for Henry, pencil neck wasn't the last, not even close. Henry couldn't bear to count them. Luckily, if there was such a thing as luck, in these situations, they were people whom he barely knew. People whose faces only stood out as blurred images from walking down the office hallway, people who maybe once or twice he had made dull small talk with. People whose upper-middle-class background and careful slog towards retirement in a job they probably hated had not prepared them for a situation like this.

As the day had gone on and gotten hotter, more of them had stripped off their life vests and jumped over the side. Following pencil neck into the cool ocean water for the last time.

"Jesus," the old first mate kept saying, each time one of them jumped over the side.

He had also given up trying to keep people from jumping overboard. Of course, there wasn't anything the survivors could do after they went over, except jump in after them, and none of them had the energy left for that. They could pull them back up the side but the jumpers never swam back, most of them like pencil neck never even tried.

The first mate repeated himself. He realized the other man was praying. Using Jesus' name as a mantra, something else to focus instead on their current surroundings. As he pulled Cheryl tighter against himself, Henry, for the first time in his life, wished he had some sort of faith. Anything to hold on to in a situation like this would be better than what they had now: nothing.

"How long does it usually take for them to find people like this?" Henry croaked to the first mate, the sound making Tim stir.

Poor Tim, who now resembled a broiled Lobster, had a mixture of dehydration seasickness, and what Henry was pretty sure was an awful hangover, now only stirred when it was time for him to shit over the side of the raft, but since bodily fluids were now a hot commodity, he was stirring less and less.

The first mate looked over at him as if seeing him for the first time. Henry waited for his response, but the look in his eyes said it all.

"It all just depends." He muttered darkly.

"Depends on what?" Henry asked again, wincing in pain. The action of trying to force words through his dry throat was more painful than he had first realized.

The first mate looked away. "Honestly, it depends on if they even know we are missing. If the captain's transmission didn't get through, then no one even knows we're out here."

"Look now, mister...?" Henry went to say but realized he didn't know the other man's name. In all the craziness, he'd forgotten to ask.

The first mate caught on. "Evans. Tyson Evans, ex-first mate of a sunken ship, and I can guess your next question easy enough." He said, looking around and seeing that now everyone aboard the life raft was hanging on to his every word. "The charter still has two more days on it, so there is little chance that anyone, crew included, will be reported missing until then. And even then, they will try to hail us first. We can only hope that they do a flyover of our last reported position. That way, we have a chance of being discovered in the water. Once they start searching, they should be able to pick up on our signal."

Tim stirred. His mouth opened, and he croaked out. "Mr. Evans, is it just me, or am I hearing a 'but' in there?" He asked, his voice sounding rougher than sandpaper and so low everyone had to strain to hear it.

Tyson looked around the raft, carefully looking every one of them in the eye. "He's not wrong. There is a 'but' in my statement. Depending on how far off we have drifted, they might not see us on their first flyover, which means we will float until they do, or until another ship gets close enough to pick us up."

"But what about the black box thing?" Cheryl asked, her voice sounding hopeful.

Tyson sighed, "It's only helpful if they know we have it. If they know that, then they can use its signal, but if they aren't looking for it, well, you know." He said with a shrug, like Atlas trying to shoulder the weight of the world.

A heavy silence descended on those in the raft. Henry himself felt it. It was as though their last bit of hope fled from them with the realization they might never be found. He saw that some others were now giving Tyson nasty looks when they thought no one was watching.

Henry wished he could be angry with the man, but he couldn't be. After all, the man was in the same situation as them. Not to mention the fact that he probably wouldn't have said anything if Henry hadn't asked him.

Now everyone's lack of hope was his fault. Seeing the utter disappointment on Cheryl's face, he certainly felt guilty.

Chapter 9

Everyone on the raft was completely silent as night fell. For Henry, the night brought its own particular brand of terror. Maybe it was a lifetime of bad late-night horror movies, but floating out here surrounded by dark water made his imagination go wild, wondering what might be swimming underneath them at any given moment, waiting to strike.

At least no one else had removed their life vests and jumped overboard. They'd already lost too many that way. On the bright side, no one else had tried to drink the saltwater either. Cheryl leaned up against him, snoring softly. Like Henry, her skin had reddened dangerously over the course of the day. By tomorrow, they'd probably all have third degree sunburn and blisters. If they didn't get rescued soon, then they'd end up dying of dehydration or sunstroke long before he had to worry about anything getting them in the water.

Compared to that, drowning on your own terms might be a better way to go. Henry thought, feeling like he might cry. But his body didn't have enough moisture left for tears.

It had finally felt like he and Cheryl were getting to a good place again and now there was a good chance he was going to have to watch her die. Henry didn't know if he could take it.

Tim moaned in his sleep from the other side of the dream. Shaken by his dark thoughts, Henry hoped his old friend was having a pleasant dream.

Tim hadn't stirred since Tyson's talk. It was like the harsh truth had sucked all the hope out of him. He also looked to be diminished somewhat, which wasn't like him at all. Tim was always the opposite of Henry: an optimist to his pessimist.

And if he felt completely beaten in this situation, then they really were in trouble. For the thousandth time, Henry wished he could do something besides just sitting on the raft and floating endlessly. Drifting off to God knows where. He wished he could...what? Swim? With a sigh, he resigned himself to knowing that his only options were to float or drown, and neither would help with their situation.

He was working a cramp out of his leg when he thought he saw something in the distance. A silhouette of something large in the water. Something with blinking lights attached to it.

A ship?

A ship, off in the distance. He couldn't make out much more than its bright lights, but, by God, he saw it. He quickly reached across the raft, feeling more energy than he had since the yacht sunk.

"Tyson! Tyson, get up!" He told him, shaking the other man with renewed vigor.

Tyson's eyes slowly cracked open. "What? What do you want now?" He asked, his voice raw and bitter.

Just like everyone else at this point, Henry thought.

Henry pointed off to the lights. "Look, over there! A ship is out there!" He all but shouted, waking up just about everyone on the raft. "Any way that we can hail it?" He asked him.

Tyson was wide awake now and together they woke the others that slept through his shouting.

"Look, we don't have a flare or any other way to signal right now, but it looks like that ship is heading our way. So, we have to use what we have. When it gets closer, we are all going to yell with all we got and splash the water loudly, anything to get their attention."

"We need to make as much noise as possible because if they don't see us...well, we just can't take the chance that another ship might pass this way." He told them, putting into words what all of them already knew deep down: this ship might just be their last chance of rescue.

They might have to swim again to get onto the ship. He realized as it got closer. It was just a big fishing boat, which meant it probably wouldn't have a smaller boat it could put overboard to pick them up.

"Look, if we have to swim, can you do it? When the time comes?" He asked Cheryl, giving her hand a reassuring squeeze as he did so.

She was wide awake looking at the ship, getting closer to them with the same hope that everyone else had. She nodded to him; her matted blonde hair swinging in front of her face as she did so. Even after almost two days adrift, Henry couldn't help but notice how beautiful she was. He wished he had told her that more before all of this had happened.

He hoped he'd be lucky enough to get the time to do it in the future.

The ship was indeed coming right at them. Soon its bright lights would fall on them and they'd be saved. At least that's what he kept telling himself.

The raft jolted violently very suddenly and sent everyone crashing into each other. Cheryl's elbow cracked into Henry's stomach with enough force to make him double over. As he helped her up, he looked over the side, looking to see if they'd struck some sort of floating debris.

"What the hell was that?" Tim asked no one in particular.

"Maybe it's just the water getting rough?" somebody replied, but Henry got a sinking feeling as he watched Tyson slowly shake his head.

"No," the first mate said.

Even Henry could tell from looking over the raft that whatever that was, the water had nothing to do with it. Another bump, this one even harder, sent the raft up on its side and let it crash back down with a splash.

Cheryl clutched at Henry for support. He held her, but no words of comfort would come to his lips. Deep down, he was terrified. Looking around, he counted there were only eight of them left now. Ten people died of dehydration and drowning. Ten faces around the office that he would never see again. For the first time, he realized how short life really was.

"Be ready to swim." He told her.

The bright lights from the ship fell on them. They were so bright that Henry had to look away. Some of the others shouted and splash in the water. Henry went to open his mouth when he suddenly fell through the air. He hadn't even gotten the opportunity to register the hard-hit that came from underneath the raft before it toppled him out into the water.

He splashed into the cold water. The salinity of it stung his eyes and made it hard to see. He heard someone gasp beside him, and he reached out. It was Cheryl. He pulled her hard toward the lights.

Whatever else was happening, he knew that was their only hope. He swam as hard as he could. His tired and cramped muscles pleaded in protest, but he pushed on, blocking out everything else.

Cheryl pulled away from him and swam beside him, both of them towards the lights.

All around them there was splashing and thrashing. More swimmers in the water. Then came the screams.

"Help! Something's-!" Came a shout that was cut off by a large splash. The sound only spurred Henry on. It was a woman's scream. He faintly remembered a pretty, young stewardess that had been on the raft with them. However, he didn't want to find out what she was screaming about.

He pushed it out of his mind. The only thing that mattered was swimming. They just had to keep swimming towards the boat, and everything would be okay, he reminded himself.

There were more screams behind them and then the sound of men shouting from the direction of the light. Loud cracks ripped across the night as Cheryl and Henry came closer to the lights.

With dim recognition, Henry realized that the men on the boat were shooting. The thought almost made him stop swimming; he thought they were shooting at them, but then in horror, he realized these men were shooting at something behind him.

But what?

Just keep swimming. He reminded himself...now more than ever, they couldn't slow down.

Finally, they made it to the side of the boat where there was already a rope ladder dangling off the side, waiting for them. Henry helped Cheryl get started and then followed up after her. Henry was pulled onto the ship by a man close to his age with straw-blonde hair, hard blue eyes, and a ragged beard: a man who, unlike Henry, looked like he knew his way around the water.

Henry and Cheryl lay gasping on the deck of the ship. Another loud crack tore through the night. Up close, the rifle made his ears ring. Cheryl pointed off to their left. There was an old man that looked a lot like the man who had pulled them aboard. Henry would bet anything that the two men were related. He stood with an old rifle snug against his shoulder, snapping out shots into the water.

Finally, the man shook his head. "I don't even think I wounded it. Is that all of them?" He asked the younger man.

The blond man nodded, and Henry realized he was talking about the others in the water. He'd been so caught up in seeing what the older man did that he hadn't realized that Tim and Tyson were now next to him and Cheryl, along with another young man, whom Henry vaguely remembered, worked in the HR department.

He also decided that after all this, he was going to introduce himself to more people. He laughed suddenly, causing Cheryl and the rest of the survivors to look at him.

"I just realized how much of a horrible introvert I am." He told them in a sudden outburst. Cheryl and Tim laughed a little at that, but the others just shrugged uncomfortably.

The blond man turned around to them. "Right, first things first. My name is Jake Taylor, and this is my father, John Taylor. This is my ship, The Angry Lady. I'm sure you all have questions and I have questions as well, but for now, let me offer the hospitality of my ship. Down below the deck is a fully functional bathroom and kitchenette stocked with water and food.

I keep it stocked for a well-fed fishing crew, so eat as much as you want. There's also coffee. Once you all are situated, then we can sit down and talk." He looked at everyone and then added, "There's also aloe gel down there for your sunburn. Damn, you all must have been out there for a while. Alright, then get to it." He said with a voice that clearly clarified that he was the captain of this ship.

Tyson stood up and headed down below, used to taking orders in the water. He snapped too with rigid familiarity. The others followed his lead, but Tim stopped short.

"What about the others that were with us?" He asked Jake.

But it was John who answered him, "They didn't make it." He said, not taking his eyes off the water, making it clear that this was a conversation for later.

Henry was too tired to care; everything hurt, and the thought of water, food, and a bath had blocked everything out of his mind. Apparently, it had for Cheryl too, since she practically pulled him below deck in glee.

Chapter 10

J ake had been in the control room when his father first spotted something floating in the water. He couldn't believe it. What they'd originally thought was just random debris turned out to be something much more.

An entire raft filled with stranded travelers.

They had spent most of the day getting out here, following the shark's known feeding patterns as best they could, but since the last attack, it had gone quiet. Making it hard for them to track. Jake almost wished for another attack just so they could catch up, almost, but deep down he wouldn't wish that kind of terror on anyone.

Then there was the storm. A freak pressure swell that had wreaked havoc on this side of the Atlantic. Luckily, they'd weathered it fine. He and his father had battened down the hatches and made it through. It had been a long night with little sleep, but they'd been lucky and had taken no damage. Other boats couldn't say the same. All morning there had been reports of missing boats.

More than a few of them had passengers and crew that had gone overboard in the rough water. Jake and his father said nothing hearing these reports. They both knew all too well the likely hood of anyone surviving on their own in the rough water.

Too many pleasure craft that hadn't prepared for the bad weather and rough water. Jake hadn't thought about going out on the water for pleasure in a long time. For him, it was about money, other than that it was the place where his nightmares lived. And now it would be that way for them, too.

The weather leading up to the storm had been beautiful and there were plenty of people who'd been taking advantage of that on small boats and ships not meant to take a beating. He wondered grimly how many of them were now lost forever.

Their job had just become that much harder. Bodies in the water meant other sharks would scavenge and the monster they were after wouldn't need to hunt to find its next meal.

It was nightfall before they made it to the floating debris. John had assumed that by following it, they'd find a much larger ship. One possibly in need of help. And while his old man was obsessed with killing the shark, neither of them could turn their backs on a ship that might be in trouble.

Out in the open water, that kind of thing just wasn't done. They'd at least check for survivors and call it into the Coast Guard, if nothing else.

As they got close enough to shine a light on what was in the water, Jake couldn't believe his eyes. In a round red life raft, sunburned and looking more than a little dehydrated, was a group of survivors.

Jake quickly altered course to come as close as safely possible up beside the raft. What ship were they from? None of them were dressed like fishermen, so the raft had to be from some sort of pleasure craft. He wondered if they'd been in the water during the storm. If so, they were lucky to be alive. Looking at them bob in the water, he wondered how many of them hadn't made it.

His father stood beside him on the deck, looking somewhat peeved.

"If we pick them up, there goes the whole hunt." He muttered darkly, looking at Jake, then back at the raft.

Jake could not believe what he was hearing. There was no way he was going to leave those people to drift. He didn't want to believe that his father was actually suggesting it. They would not survive without help, and who knew when another ship might happen by? If Jake left them, he was killing them. It was as simple as that.

No, he would not take that on his conscience. Enough people had already died because of the shark.

"Look, shark or no shark, we are getting those people on board." He told his father in a voice that left no room for argument. It was the same voice that he used when giving orders to his crew.

For the first time, he worried about what lengths his father was willing to go to when it came to the shark. He decided right then that he didn't want to find out.

Looking out at the raft, he could see something was wrong even before his father started yelling.

The people on the raft had stopped trying to get their attention. Instead, they were looking around wildly and clutching the sides of the large raft. Which was now bouncing around in the water as though something was ramming it from underneath.

What are they looking at? He wondered, fear gripping him as he watched the all too familiar scene play out. Is that how it looked when he and his brother got attacked?

His father had run below deck to grab weapons, and Jake had gone ahead and dropped the anchors. The Angry Lady bucked a little as they caught hold below.

It was for the best; he decided. Besides, if he had tried to get even closer to the raft, he would be risking the safety of those on it. The raft was close enough now where they could swim as long as they could stay ahead of the man-eater, now circling, waiting for them to be brave enough to try.

He grabbed the rope ladder on the way out of the control room. It was something he had kept on the ship out of necessity and hoped he'd never actually had to use. Two large metal hooks kept it fastened to whichever side of the ship it was needed on.

Without wasting time, he hooked it over to the side and listened as the bottom stair splashed in the water. Whatever had the people in the raft so scared had hit them again. This time coming close to sending a couple of them over the side. His heart pounded in his chest watching the scene in front of him. It was like he was back on the buoy all over again. A helpless, terrified child, unable to save the people in front of him.

A loud thump behind him let him know his father was back from below deck. He was carrying a large bolt-action rifle. One that he was loading while he ran.

His father caught his look and said, "Something's bumping around their raft."

"You don't think it's our shark, do you?" He asked in shock. Jake suddenly as he gripped the side of the rails, unable to look away from the raft. He'd hoped it was something else, anything else at this point. But, deep down, he'd known exactly what was trying to flip over the raft and why.

"It fits the pattern, and it's on the same path." His father muttered, working the bolt-action and racking a round into the chamber.

Everything happened so fast, Jake could hardly believe what he saw when the raft was suddenly hit again, this time sending it careening into the air.

"Holy sh-!" He heard his father start, but he couldn't hear anything else besides the blood pounding in his ears.

The raft sailed up into the air as something massive hit it from underneath. Jake wasn't sure if it was a trick or his eyes seeing what he wanted to see, but he swore that even from where he stood, he could see the shark as it flipped the raft.

And it was the same monster that had haunted his nightmares for so many years. No matter how much he tried to tell himself otherwise, he'd never forget what that shark looked like. Not until the day he died.

The survivors from the raft started swimming towards the boat, ignorant of the shark and the danger they were in. Not for long though, the shark quickly descended upon the people in the water, and then the real screaming began.

Jake felt powerless as he saw the people in the water struggle in vain, only to be pulled down by the shark's powerful jaws.

Suddenly, there was a loud crack that left his ears ringing. Followed by another.

"Watch out for the people in the water!" Jake shouted to his father, as the old man fired one shot after another, pausing only when he had to reload.

"I see them. I see them." He replied, not looking up from the butt of the rifle.

Jake hoped maybe they would get lucky and one of his father's shots would end the beast's miserable life. At most, it might scare it off and buy some swimmers the time they needed to reach the boat.

From the side of the railing, he heard a loud clang as the hooks were pulled tight and quickly leaned over to help the survivors as they climbed up.

They were completely dazed as he hauled them over: a man and a woman, then three others behind them. They waited, but no one else came over the side. The water had become eerily silent. Looking at it now with the moon shining over, he could almost forget the violence that had just occurred.

The vision of tranquility was shattered, however, when his eyes fell on the still floating redraft. Now upside down. A reminder that even though they had saved some, the shark had feasted tonight on too many people. While they were once again powerless to stop it.

"I don't think I even winged the damned thing." His father muttered, his face a mask of disappointment as he dropped the rifle from his shoulder.

The survivors were rising slowly to their feet. Jake didn't know how he would break it to them, but until they put an end to that shark's life, none of them were going home.

Because after seeing that kind of carnage, what the shark was truly capable of, he couldn't shake the feeling that it was only getting started.

Chapter 11

Henry's skin was already cracking and blisters were rising over the uncovered parts of his body, but at least his legs were no longer cramped in that tiny raft. With a contented sigh, he stretched out. Content with the stretching and popping sounds they made, he practically groaned with pleasure. More than happy to be free of the raft and the shark waiting for them in the water.

God, he couldn't wait to go home, take a shower, sleep in his own bed next to his wife, and push this complete nightmare of a trip out of his mind forever.

Above him, Cheryl rolled over in her sleep, making their shared bunk bed creak. It had to be around noon now, gauging from the light coming down the stairs, but he wasn't sure. After chugging water, eating and partaking in the captain's hospitality, they'd gone straight to bed. He'd been so exhausted he'd fallen asleep as soon as his head hit the bunk.

Henry finally felt like a person again. A starving person, he realized as his stomach rumbled. Hopefully, soon they would be home and they could eat a proper meal, but until then, he'd have to eat the canned food and rations that Captain Taylor kept on hand.

When they got back, he was going to talk to Cheryl about moving. He didn't want to live in spitting distance of the water anymore. Mountains maybe, or a desert, would be a pleasant change.

He'd thought about moving on and off for years and besides, Tim had been saying for a while now that he could work from home if he wanted to. Now seemed like a good time to take him up on that offer.

He tossed and turned several more times before he realizing that he wasn't going back to sleep anytime soon. He'd wanted to put off eating until he got back, but it didn't look like it was going to happen.

"Damn," He muttered to himself and carefully got out of the bunk, doing his best not to wake Cheryl as he did so.

With what they'd been through, they needed all the sleep they could get. Everything in his body ached as he stood up. Henry couldn't remember the last time he'd had to do anything physically active.

Cheryl at least had kept up with her weekly Yoga, whereas he'd done absolutely nothing but go to work and come home the last few years. Too tired to do anything more than eat dinner and make small talk with his wife.

He still couldn't believe everything that had happened. First, the yacht they were on sinks in a storm, something he still didn't completely understand. Though knowing Tim, he'd probably booked them on the cheapest cruise he could find, maybe they'd get a settlement when they got back. As soon as the thought went through his mind, he felt guilty, remembering all the people that had died.

And then there was the shark.

For the first time, he thought about what they were going to tell people. So many people were dead; someone or something would have to answer for that if nothing else. Sharks didn't just attack people like that, at least he thought they didn't. One thing was for sure: he wouldn't get back into the water to find out.

Henry made his way from the bunk area to the galley. There he found Tyson and Tim sitting together talking in low voices, but Henry was more concerned about the empty plates sitting in front of them, and the smell of coffee.

Wasting no time in getting himself a cup, he quickly stirred in his sugar, savoring the heady aroma of the dark brew. Though he couldn't help but ask, "Has the Captain said how soon we'll get back to shore?"

Tim shook his head and Henry noticed Tyson looked somewhat worried, but he didn't know why.

"No, the Captain hasn't said much of anything to any of us since breakfast and neither has the old man." He said, and then as if an afterthought, "There's still some powdered eggs left if you want some."

"Okay, thanks," Henry replied, quickly getting back up and making himself a small plate. He took half of what was left. That way, there would be some for Cheryl when she got up.

They were cold, and he had never liked eggs much, but after all he'd been through, he didn't care. He barely tasted them as he shoveled them into his mouth, hoping to stop grumbling in his stomach.

"So, if the captain hasn't said anything, why the long faces?" He asked, looking at Tyson in particular.

"Tyson thinks we're headed back out to sea," Tim said, glaring at the other man.

"That's not what I said," Tyson stammered. "What I said was that while we are heading back into the bay from the ocean, we aren't heading to any ports or marinas."

"How can you tell?" Henry asked, nervously tapping his fingers against the table.

Tyson shrugged. "Because if he were, he'd have done it by now. I've been running with ships in and out of the bay and into the Atlantic all my life. Long before I was the first mate on that pleasure yacht, no, the captain's got no interest in taking us to shore, at least not yet. Whatever they're doing out here, they don't want to be stopped."

Tim groaned, as if not wanting to relive this conversation, but Henry was intrigued. "But why do you think that is? Come on, tell me?" He asked almost pleadingly.

Tyson looked away again and then stared into his half-empty cup of coffee. Clearly uncomfortable with his own speculation. "This is a decent-sized fishing ship made for going staying in deep water, days in the bay or along the Atlantic. But if it were being used for fishing now, it would have a larger crew than two men, and ships like this aren't cheap to run. Every day this thing is out here, it's costing someone a lot of money in fuel. So, the question is, what are they doing out here?

I mean, this ship is stocked for at least a week or more's worth of travel, and they've got rifles. All I'm saying is...I don't think they picked us up because of the GPS, but I don't think them running into us was an accident, either."

Henry shrugged, his body ached, and his head hurt. The last thing he wanted to try was to play guessing games. "I don't know. What do you think they were doing out there?" He asked, looking around to make sure the captain and the old man were still above deck.

Tim slammed his hand down on the table, making them all jump.

"He thinks they were out here hunting the shark. Like Captain Ahab after their Moby Dick!" He growled. " And it's stupid! The last thing we need right now is to hear that kind of crap. We've been through enough without having to worry about our rescuer's motives."

Tim moved, and Henry stood to let him out of the booth. "I'm going back to see if Aaron's awake." He said, walking back in the direction of the bunk areas. Aaron must have been the other guy who made it from the raft. Henry felt terrible because, like most of his coworkers and the crew of the yacht, he didn't know who the man was. It was like until the trip he'd been living his life in some sort of fugue state.

Henry and Tyson watched him leave. Already they could see where Tim was peeling. At least he looked a little less red, more than a few of the blisters had popped and were oozing down his back and face. Henry wondered how long it would take his to do the same and shuddered.

Maybe that was what had him so irritable, Henry thought, realizing that he should also probably be losing his shit about now, but found that he couldn't. With all that had happened, and how fast it had happened, well, to be honest, none of it felt real yet.

He and Tyson finished their coffee in relative silence, broken only by the occasional grunts of appreciation after every sip. Cheryl woke up a little after Tim had stormed off and finished the rest of the powdered eggs. The other man, Aaron, would just have to fend for himself.

Cheryl looked a lot better, certainly less sunburned than Tim and him; Henry realized she seemed to be, in some way renewed. He couldn't put his finger on it, but all he wanted to do at that moment was wrap his arms around her, take her to bed and celebrate being alive. And from the way she pressed against him and the familiar looks she gave him, it was clear Cheryl wanted to do the same.

Instead, he got up and put his dishes away.

"I'm going to go up and talk to the captain," Henry told them. "That way, instead of speculating, maybe we can get a straight answer."

Tyson shrugged as if to say good luck with that. And Cheryl just smiled at him, then went back to eating. They had filled her in on what had happened while she slept. All she said was that as long as they were on this boat and not floating in a damn raft, she could care less as long as they got home at some point.

Henry made his way up to the deck. He was happy that he had found his sea legs, after all. He hadn't noticed it until now. The rocking and rolling of the water no longer made him sick or tripped him up.

The old man was on the deck with a pair of binoculars in his hands. Henry hadn't gotten a good look at him last night, but now he could see the family resemblance; right down to the sharp blue eyes and dark, tanned skin that bespoke of a lifetime spent on the water.

"Where's the captain?" He asked him.

John Taylor never even put down his binoculars, opting instead to continue scanning the water. Henry was afraid to ask what it was he was looking for. He felt like he had a good idea. Maybe the others were right after all.

"He's up in the control room. Steering the ship." John replied.

Henry left John to his vigil and went up the narrow metal stairs to the control room. He knocked on the door.

"Come in," Jake said, his voice easily heard over the sounds of the ocean and the engines of the ship.

Henry walked in, standing closer to the door. Jake was seated in a large leather chair in front of a wheel with tons of radars, switches, and knobs. Henry didn't even want to try and guess what they all did.

"You wanted something?" Jake asked him; he looked much the same as he had the night before.

Henry doubted the man had even changed his clothes, or slept for that matter.

Had he left his post at all? Henry wondered and realized quickly that he might not like that answer either.

Jake looked at him, waiting impatiently for Henry to ask whatever it was he had on his mind.

Henry cleared his throat and looked straight into Jake's stormy blue eyes. "I wanted to thank you for saving us last night." He started hoping to soften the blow before he asked his real question.

Jake sighed. "Think nothing of it. I'm just happy we were in the area." He replied.

"Did you all manage to kill the shark that attacked the raft?" He asked. From the look on Jake's face, it appeared he'd asked the wrong question.

Finally, Jake just shrugged. "No, I don't even think we winged it. The only way we are going to know for sure that shark is dead is to drag it on board and do the deed with our own hands." He said with a pained expression on his face.

The way he said it confirmed Henry's fears. "You have no intention of bringing us back to shore, do you?"

Jake turned back to him. "I have every intention of making sure you all make it safely back to shore, but first I have matters to attend to out here. And until then, you are welcome to roam freely about The Angry Lady. While it might not be a yacht or some other pleasure craft, it has most of the creature comforts you will need. And when I am finished with my business, we will head into the bay and to the nearest marina, where we will signal the Coast Guard and let them know of your situation."

The sinking feeling in Henry's gut seemed to deepen. "And your business? That's hunting down the shark, isn't it? That's why you don't want the Coast Guard to know about us and why you won't take us back now. You don't want to answer their questions as to why you were out there."

Jake smiled. "Well, I'm glad you put it all together. You're right, I don't want to answer questions, so please leave. Enjoy your stay on my ship and close the door behind you." He said evenly.

Henry complied and as the control room door shut behind him, he wondered how he was going to break the news to the others.

Chapter 12

After talking to the Captain, Henry had gone back down below to sit in the shade with the others and relay what he'd been told. He was glad to be off the raft, but he couldn't shake the feeling that they'd traded one dangerous situation for another. Not that he thought Captain Taylor, or his father would harm them, but he didn't want to stay out here any longer than they had to. And the Captain had made it clear that they weren't leaving the water until they got their shark.

What if they never did?

They were obsessed and Henry didn't even want to speculate on how far they would go to get their prize.

This all felt like some sort of strange nightmare.

Yet, no matter how many times he pinched himself, he was still here, stuck on a fishing boat in the Atlantic Ocean.

The others seemed to feel the same way. Tyson mainly talked to Aaron, who they all quickly discovered was nothing more than a pencil-necked kiss-ass. Henry was glad he hadn't been friendlier with the man back in the office. The only thing Henry couldn't figure out was why Aaron had latched onto Tyson, but whatever the reason, he knew it couldn't be good. The man was a shit-stirrer, plain and simple. Henry had seen his type before and their situation was dire enough without someone stirring the pot.

And then there was Tim.

Well, Tim did nothing. He seemed to have resigned himself to the fact that Captain Taylor wasn't going straight back to shore and had opted to sleep the rest of the day. He barely even talked.

Henry had only glimpsed the man when he came out to eat or use the bathroom. Other than that, Tim lay on his bunk bundled up under blankets. Tim's demeanor on the few occasions he left his cocoon had been completely disheartening. The amiable smile and optimism that Henry had always gotten from his friend had vanished. Tim looked like he'd aged ten years and seemed like a husk of his former self.

Henry just hoped that with time, Tim would be okay. He hoped they'd all be okay.

Henry was lucky. Through this whole thing, Cheryl had been his rock. Not with words. No, they had talked little after they were cast adrift and barely at all after the rescue. It was her presence; it was the little reassuring pats and squeezes. Little things she did that let him know for sure that things could be normal once again. She, too, had spent most of the day in her bunk, but he couldn't blame her. There really wasn't anything for them to do on this ship, other than stay out of the way.

What was really nagging Henry, though, as he sat alone at the booth and heard the constant whispering coming from Tyson and Aaron from back in the galley, was that he felt useless.

On this fishing boat, he was just sitting here, not doing a damn thing while above deck, two men now held all their fates resting in the palms of their callused hands. Mustering up his courage, he walked past him and Cheryl's bunk. She waved at him as he walked by. She had found a couple of old paperback books and was keeping herself busy with them.

He stood on the other side of Tim's bunk. "Tim, get up." He said.

He knew Tim was awake since he heard movement from behind the curtain that acted as a door. The bunk creaked as Tim sat up.

"Tim, get up. You can't just lie around all afternoon."

The pile of blankets moved, and Henry heard Tim's feet hitting the floor. As he stood, Tim dropped the blankets back on the bunk.

Tim was so red that Henry couldn't tell if he was angry or not. If it had been any other time, Henry would have made a joke about his old friend's appearance, but clearly, the other man was in pain. Henry could practically see the peeling skin falling off of him as he moved.

When Tim spoke, he didn't sound angry, just defeated. "What is it we are supposed to do?" He asked.

Henry smiled at him. "Go fishing."

Tim was clearly shocked, but only for a moment. Then his look of confusion was replaced with a hard frown, one filled with grim determination. Henry had been right; they both needed this. He had wanted to talk to Tyson about it, but the other man had shut the rest of them out. The only person he was talking to now was Aaron.

Tim followed Henry up the stairs, back onto the deck. John was up there, his eyes piercing the horizon in a constant vigil. He stopped staring out into the water only long enough to check the lines on either side of the ship. He looked over at them as they walked up only briefly as they came up to the deck.

"Do you need a hand?" Henry asked him.

If the old man was surprised he didn't show it. Maybe he'd already assumed that it was bound to happen. After all, being hunted through the water by a shark and listening as it ate people you slightly knew would give most people a reason to want it dead, and if not, the boredom of being on a ship with nothing to do would.

"Yeah, go hack up some chum. Don't get fancy with it, just fill the buckets." John told them gruffly, pointing a thumb over to an already bloody cutting board. Several empty buckets sat near it.

The fish they needed to cut up were frozen, and Henry found it to be a messy, smelly job, but at least it got their minds off of their situation. Watching Tim hack away at the frozen fish with an old hatchet, he couldn't believe that he had been so dumb.

Of course, Tim was more upset about this than he was. Tim had known all of those people on a personal level. Unlike Henry, who'd kept his co-workers at arm's length. They weren't just blurred faces in the hallway for him.

Tim used to make fun of Henry for not knowing everyone's name while Tim had known all of them. He'd prided himself on it. That was always one of the big differences between them. While Henry had looked at the office as just a job, a place he came to do his time and make a little money, Tim had loved it, saw it as a career, and felt responsible for everything that had happened.

"Hey, man, look if you need to talk or anything, well, I'm here, okay?" Henry told him awkwardly, without looking up from hacking up a fish with the large butcher knife. He couldn't have looked up if he had wanted to, at least not without risking his fingers.

"I'll be fine. It's just it doesn't feel real, you know?" Tim said with a snort. "I mean, between the storm, being set adrift on a raft, and then being attacked by a shark, can this get any worse?" He asked.

Both men looked off in the distance, half expecting to see lightning flashing in the distance. They looked at each other and gave a soft chuckle before going back to work.

In no time, they had all the buckets full. John showed them how to chum the waters. They would only throw some overboard every now and again, just to draw in whatever predators might swim close by. Once they were close, they might decide to bite one of the many lines John had sitting out.

After a while, John relieved them of their duties. John had a way he wanted it done, and they were happy to leave him to it. They sat on the deck and took a break, checking the lines sporadically and making sure they were around if John needed any more help.

Shortly after checking the lines, they sat back down. Tyson and Aaron stormed up the stairs onto the deck. One look at the pair and Henry could tell that trouble was brewing.

They went right up to the control room. Henry, Tim and John all exchanged. The old man also apparently picked up on the fact that something was up. He shrugged, apparently deciding that whatever they were up to, it wasn't his problem. The ship slowed a little and Jake came down, with Tyson and Aaron trailing behind them. He lifted open a hatch on the deck and inflated a small inflatable raft. Not like the massive one they were on. No, this one was more like a dinghy. He also pulled out a small prop engine.

"I want it on the record that this is madness. You two realize that we have been chumming the water for a man-eating shark for most of the day, right? Not to mention the fact that you will be in the ocean on this with miles between you and the bay, one harsh wind, and you won't make the Virginia coast by nightfall." Jake said to them, pointing at the raft for emphasis.

Tyson held up his hands. "Look, we are close enough to the mouth of the bay. I can get us that far, no problem. Once in the bay, we hit the nearest patch of land and walk to the nearest phone." He replied. Aaron just nodded.

Henry and Tim said nothing. When Jake looked over at him, all Henry could do was shrug. It was their funeral. They all helped to get the raft off the side and steadied the rope ladder as they climbed into it. Once both of the men were in, they handed the prop down to Tyson. He waved to them with a weak smile on his face as he set up the little engine at the back of the raft.

"See you all on the other side." He called out to them as the prop fired up. They all stood on the deck and watched them leave. The raft pushed its way through the water at a decent speed. Henry hoped it would be enough.

Soon they were just little dots on the horizon, barely visible in the afternoon sun.

Jake shook his head and ran a hand through his beard. He knew that the tiredness he was feeling was more than physical.

"Idiots," He muttered and walked back into his control room.

His father only shrugged.

Tim and Henry stood there, not knowing what to do.

Henry wished them the best, but they should have waited. Yeah, sure, he would love to be back on land as much as they would, but for Tyson to up and try to navigate a dingy back to land was foolhardy. Especially since the sun would be down in the next couple of hours.

Maybe he didn't know as much about the ocean as Tyson and the Taylors did, but Tyson should have known better than to risk both their lives.

"God helps those who help themselves, hopefully." He said, shaking his head. Tim looked up at him, confused.

"Maybe that's what they were thinking when they made that plan." He told him.

"When did you get religious?" Tim asked him.

Henry shrugged his shoulders. Neither one of them had to guess the answer to that question.

The ship's intercom blared over the deck, "Pull up the lines!" Jake's voice echoed out over the deck, followed by static crackling.

John looked irritated and like he was about to give Jake a piece of his mind.

Jake's voice echoed out again, "There's been another one," was all it said.

"Shit," Cursed John.

"What is it?" Tim and Henry asked in unison as they helped him get the lines out of the water.

"He means there's been another shark attack," John told them and went back to muttering to himself.

Chapter 13

A few miles away from *The Angry Lady*, Chad and his friends were getting good and drunk. They had his dad's speedboat, girls, and enough booze to send a person to the hospital. To Chad, the night was shaping up to be one hell of a good night. Fist-bumping his friend Donny, he turned off the engines and let the boat drift.

They were just a little way out of the bay, far enough that they could say they were in the ocean, but close enough to shore that it wasn't dangerous. That way, if anything happened, or they got a little too intoxicated, they could follow the shoreline back.

Chad wasn't stupid enough to take his dad's boat out further than that.

It was a good little spot for them to hang out without going into the much deeper and rougher water. Plus, out here, they didn't have to worry about hitting a crab pot in the dark.

Jackie and Amy stripped down to their bathing suits. Chad took a swig of his dad's pilfered beer and gave Donny another fist bump as they both watched. Neither of them even pretending to look elsewhere.

He'd seen the girls around school before, but up until now, they'd never actually hung out. Right now, he was glad he'd let Donny talk him into taking his dad's boat for a joyride. Sure, he might catch shit later. But, one look over at the two tanned, toned bodies on the other end of the boat and Chad didn't have a care in the world.

How Donny had pulled this off and get them to agree to come out. He had no clue, but he owed him one. Amy caught him staring and gave him a smile and a wink.

Chad blushed and gave her a pathetic little wave in return. Donny turned the radio on, not rock like they usually listened to. No, this was way more pop-sounding, but he couldn't argue it was a good choice because soon everyone started drinking and dancing.

Jackie pressed herself up close against Donny as they danced. If you could call it that, Chad thought, watching them both grind away at each other in a way that left nothing to the imagination about what they really wanted to do.

"Eyes on me," Amy whispered to him while grinding her body against his to the music while the boat rocked with the waves.

All thoughts of Jackie and Donny fled his mind. He slipped his hands over her tight, tan waist and did his best to keep up. The sweet coconut smell coming from her auburn hair seemed to cloud his mind, and she was all he could think about. That and the way her body moved against his teasingly, Chad didn't want this song to ever end.

"I want to go swimming!" Jackie suddenly shouted and grabbed Amy, pulling her away from him.

So much for his good time. He sighed as she and Jackie went to the back of the boat.

Amy gave him a small smile as she and Jackie went to the back of the boat and jumped off. Donny looked at them and then at him, shrugged, and pulled off his shirt off. Then he took a running leap that ended in an enormous splash, making the girls in the water squeal.

Chad was about to follow suit when he remembered the little ladder on the side of the boat. Thankful that for once he'd listened to something his father had told him, he released it and sent it down into the water. It would have been nearly impossible for them to get it to drop while swimming, and without it, they wouldn't be able to get back on board.

From the water, Amy waggled her fingers seductively for him to join her. Jackie and Donny were already splashing around and pawing at one another. Chad wasn't the least bit jealous though, he just hoped he'd get to do the same with Amy.

He swallowed and looked at her, letting his courage build. To be honest, Chad hated deep water and by that, he meant any water that he couldn't see his feet in. He also hated the idea of swimming in the dark; something about it to him had always just seemed like asking for trouble.

But Amy was already in the water, and she was beautiful and, for some reason, she seemed to like him. Which meant that no matter how much he didn't want to, he was getting in the water because if he didn't, Chad knew he'd regret the decision for the rest of his life.

A quick dip couldn't hurt, could it? He asked himself.

Besides, it wasn't like he was going to plead with them to get back on the boat. No way, he didn't want to be that guy. He chugged the rest of his beer for a little additional courage, wishing that he could get a little more of buzz going, for bravery if nothing else.

Amy gestured again and Chad pulled off his shirt, hoping the night would make his farmer's tan look less pale, and he jumped. He almost let his breath out when his head went underwater. The water was freezing cold. He hoped his body would acclimate soon if not, then he wouldn't have to worry about having any fun with Amy.

"Over here!" He heard Amy say as he spat the salt water out of his mouth and tried in vain to rub it out of his eyes.

He swam blindly toward her voice. Warm hands suddenly wrapped around him and her body pressed against his. Just like that, Chad no longer cared about the salt water in his eyes or being in the water for that matter.

"Hey," he said, feeling the heat rise to his face and hoping she wouldn't be able to see him blush.

Her arms were still around him.

"Hey," she replied, moving her lips onto his.

Chad kissed her back and as her breasts pushed up against his chest, he almost forgot to keep treading water, and they both started to sink. At some point, she had wrapped her legs around him, and somehow he remembered to keep them both afloat.

They broke apart briefly, laughing.

"Should we move this party back on the boat?" Chad asked, hoping his voice didn't crack when did.

Amy giggled. "Sure." She said and took his hand as they swam back to the boat.

Chad was preoccupied with helping and ogling Amy at the same time as she climbed up the ladder. Her tight purple bikini left nothing to the imagination, which was fine with him. Chad was tired of his imagination, anyway.

Just as Chad put his first foot on the step to climb out, Jackie screamed from behind him. A loud, blood-curdling shriek. People didn't scream like that, not if they were just joking around. That thought kept bouncing around his brain as he stood frozen on the ladder, still halfway submerged in the water.

He could see her then. Jackie. She was swimming fast towards the boat. He dimly remembered Donny saying something about her being on the swim team or something like that at school, watching her easily push through the water like a human torpedo he believed it.

Looking around, he didn't see Donny, which was weird. The way those two were all over each other, he couldn't imagine his friend letting her out of his sight. Shit, Chad thought, hoping that Donny hadn't tried something weird and just ruined the whole night for both of them.

Someone was still shouting. It was Jackie.

"Start the boat! Start the boat!" shouting the phrase like a mantra as she swam towards him.

The panic in her voice helped to snap him out of his thoughts. Chad climbed the rest of the way up the ladder and went to the front, then he turned the key. Amy sat on the bench seat in the back. She looked frightened as she watched her friend swim towards the ladder, and he couldn't blame her.

"What's happening?" She asked him.

"I don't know," was all he could say. Now more than a little worried about Donny, who he couldn't see anywhere in the water. He wished Jackie would hurry and get aboard so they could find out what the hell's going on.

The engines idled, and they both turned around to see Jackie. For just a moment, it looked like there was something in the water behind her, but she was almost at the ladder. He figured it had to be the beer or the fact that they were out here at night because he could swear that what he was seeing was a large fin.

Was Donny pulling a prank?

His friend loved that kind of shit, but he had seen him get in the water wearing nothing but trunks. No matter how much of an asshole Donny could be at times, Chad knew he wouldn't do anything to screw up his chances with a girl like Jackie. Not on purpose, anyway.

He leaned over the side to help grab Jackie's outstretched hand. He had just grabbed hold of her when something rose behind her. There was a lot of screaming then. His hers, probably Amy's too. Chad did not believe what he was seeing. It was a shark, and a big one at that. It appeared right behind Jackie, its cruel teeth snapping down on the lower half of her body just as he was pulling her on board.

He tried to hold on, but he just wasn't strong enough. The whole time he was staring into the cold, black eyes of the shark as it pulled Jackie back down into the water.

He grabbed a flashlight and ran back. When he flipped its switch, he instantly wished that he hadn't; the water was dark red. Just as he was about to turn back around, Jackie broke the surface, screaming. "He-!" She started when the shark hit her again, this time driving her against the boat and splashing them with gore.

"Oh my God!" Amy screamed. "Jackie!"

Still shaking, Chad shined his flashlight over the side again. This time, no one broke the surface. He tried not to look at the blood on the side of the boat, or on his chest.

Amy was sobbing, and he was shaking. He wanted to lie down and let all of this be a bad dream. No, wait; there was something he could do. He grabbed the radio and pressed the side until he heard static. Then sent out a distress call, reading the GPS location off just like his dad had shown him how to do in case of emergency. And this was definitely an emergency.

Then he took a deep breath and said, "Shark attack!"

Hopefully, someone would hear and take it seriously.

"Let's get out of here, please," Amy said, coming to sit beside him on the captain's seat. She was warm, and he enjoyed being close to her. He slid closer to her, taking comfort in the fact that he wasn't going through this alone. Chad also didn't know if they could leave. Two of their friends were missing. Surely someone would get back to them on the radio, wouldn't they?

After a couple of minutes, he switched off the blaring radio. The static was too loud and had made him more than a little anxious. Now the night was eerily silent; only broken by the small waves that rocked the boat. Looking out at the night, it felt sinister and dangerous. Amy was right they needed to get out of here.

Chad realized solemnly that they'd just fallen a notch on the food chain, and he didn't like it.

"Hold on a minute, just, please, let me try this really quick." He pleaded, knowing that he owed it to Donny and Jackie to make one last attempt. Amy nodded, looking as if at any minute she might collapse in on herself. He didn't know what to do if she went into shock. He and Donny had stopped at Cub Scouts, so all his medical knowledge stopped after get an adult.

"Donny!" Chad shouted a few times from the back of the boat. Hoping that his friend would resurface, even though deep down he already knew the truth.

Only silence answered him. Amy was right; they had to leave. He didn't understand how this had happened, or how they were going to explain it. Amy tugged him back to the console. "He's gone... okay, he's gone, and we have to go now!"

Chad sat down, wondering if they should leave wasn't that illegal? What if someone came who could help them?

The first thump underneath the boat was all the encouragement he needed. With Amy holding on to him tightly, he gunned the engine, letting the nimble speedboat fly across the water, its nose dangerously high in the air. He was driving it the same way his dad did when he wanted to show off and had already drunk a few too many.

Shit, he was going too fast. He needed to slow down. The last thing he wanted was to get them both killed in a boating accident. Plus, he could barely see ahead of them as the boat lights weren't that bright, and the nose was too high up.

Something jerked them back as they made their way into the bay. Shit. He had snagged a damn crab pot.

Amy looked at him like he was crazy when he brought the boat down to an idle and killed the engines.

"What the hell are you doing?" She asked, cradling herself. Tears ran freely down her face. He wanted nothing more than to wipe them off and tell her everything was going to be okay, but they didn't have time. And deep down, Chad didn't know if anything would ever be okay again.

"If I don't get that rope loose, it will break the prop. If it's not already tangled in it, I should just be able to raise the prop.

Hopefully, then it will slide off. If not, I'll cut the rope." He replied, not adding that he might have to get in the water to do it.

"How will you know?" She asked him.

Chad nervously cleared his throat. "Normally, my dad would make me get in the water to check, but fuck that." He told her, seeing Jackie's outstretched hand in his mind right before it dragged her under. He shuddered.

"So instead, I'm going to lean off of the side and check it. Can you hold my legs?"

She nodded. He pulled out the little hunting knife his dad always kept on the boat. It was a little rusty from the constant exposure to saltwater, but he prayed it would do the job. Leaning over the side, he gulped as he came closer to its fathomless depths.

With his face only inches away and his hands now in the water, Amy held his legs, clamping them tightly with her full weight against the boat. With the knife clutched tightly between his teeth, Chad felt around until he found the prop.

To his relief, it was good. The engine had snagged the line, but it hadn't become twisted up in the propeller as he'd feared. With one hand, he took the knife out of his mouth and called back.

"Hey, pull me-," He didn't get to finish; there was a heavy pressure followed by a pull on his right hand which still clutched the knife.

He looked down at the culprit. Being so close, he could make out its football-shaped head. It was massive, but it wasn't a great white. He knew that much from his high school oceanography class, he didn't know why that was important.

Chad wondered if he was in shock. His arm hurt as it kept swimming past him, going under the boat. There was a sharp searing pain, and then he was aware of the blood pouring down his arm from the place where his hand used to be.

Someone was screaming.

Maybe Amy.

Maybe him. He wasn't sure none of it felt real anymore.

Just as soon as it appeared, the shark had vanished. Amy pulled him back away from the water. At least he thought she did. He couldn't help it; he couldn't look at anything except for the place where his hand used to be.

Amy was crying and screaming about something as she wrapped his bleeding stump tightly in a beach towel.

"How do I start the boat?!" She kept screaming at him and smacking his face. Her words finally sunk in.

"Turn the key." He said. Chad realized he sounded funny, and that he was very light-headed suddenly. Heavily, he sat down and tried to keep his eyes open. The entire world seemed just a bit hazy.

Of course, I sound funny. I just lost my hand to a shark. He started to laugh.

Amy turned the key, and the engines started. She threw the boat into gear and launched off. Too late, Chad realized he'd never got it unstuck. The line hit the propeller and there was a loud sounding boom as the prop was yanked backward. The engines cut off and smoke started to billow out of it.

The boat had been going too fast and who knew what they had messed up in the engine. Amy turned back to stare at them. Even though the boat was still going forward, she never even saw the green water level sign when it popped out in front of them. Not that they could have slowed down in time, anyway. Chad saw it right before the front of the boat smashed into it.

He suddenly found that his whole body was cold and wet.

I'm in the water, he thought dimly.

Blood loss was affecting him. The moon lit the water, making everything dimly visible. Something big was swimming towards him. He noticed his stump was sending up a small dark cloud. The beach towel was gone, and he could make out the glimmer of bone in the moonlight.

As the dark shape got closer, Chad tried to swim away, but the agile fins quickly outpaced him in their native environment. Chad's last thought was to try and warn Amy as he felt that ungodly pressure again, first on his leg as the shark pulled him further down... then on his chest as it tore away a chunk, followed by another.

Chad could only watch as the shark tore into him again and again.

It may have bitten him in more places, but he was past the point of feeling such things.

Chapter 14

B y the time *The Angry Lady* got to the scene of the accident, they were already too late. The only sign that anyone had even been out was a half-submerged speedboat which was quickly taking on water, and slowly disappearing out of sight.

There wasn't a single person in sight.

"What kind of shark could do this?" Tim asked loudly as they all clamored around the deck of the ship. Each of them looking and hoping to see a survivor. Though Henry very much doubted they would. If anyone was still alive, they would have seen them by now.

Cheryl had joined them on the deck and Henry threw his arms around her as they watched the smaller boat sink further and further down into the water until it was almost out of sight.

It was John who answered Tim's question as they all moved their handheld flashlights back and forth looking unsuccessfully for any signs of life.

"The shark didn't do that," Jake said, motioning towards the sinking boat. "They sounded like scared kids over the radio. They must have run into that pylon. That's what caused all the damage." He told them, pointing out the cracked wooden beam, which was now barely visible in the water. "See orange thing bobbing in the water? That's a marker for crab pots. My guess is they hooked it, and then ran the boat into the pylon."

"But what kind of shark are we after?" Henry ventured. "I mean, what could do this? This isn't the Pacific Ocean, so it can't be a Great White or anything like that, right?"

John coughed and spat out into the water. "No, it ain't a Great White. I've never laid eyes on it personally," He said, giving Jake a look, "But if I had to guess, what we are after is a Bull Shark. They can get up to 10ft long and up to a thousand pounds. What most people don't realize is that they're one of the more aggressive species sharks on the planet."

"But how can you know?" Cheryl asked, turning away from the sinking boat.

"I've been researching it since the damn thing turned one of my boys into a Happy Meal. Guess that makes me close enough to an expert." He replied.

"Oh my God, I'm so sorry." Cheryl quickly apologized. Henry rubbed the back of his neck, not knowing what to say. He'd known the father and sons need to get the shark was personal. He just hadn't realized it was that personal.

But John wasn't quite through yet. "I read everything about sharks I could get my hands on, and I asked around, working on boats you get to hear things, things that don't make the news and I studied every article. You see, it's not uncommon for bull sharks to come up into bays and rivers. Places most people would never expect to see a shark.

They can even survive for a time in freshwater. That means not even lakes are safe. Like all sharks, they migrate from colder to warmer water. That's how I got the pattern, you see, somewhere along the line, this shark got wise. It realized that it didn't have to chase after fish or fight others over whatever dead meat it came across.

No, this shark realized that there was slower, dumber prey in its waters, prey it could easily outpace in its natural habitat." He said, staring at each of them to add emphasis.

"Wait," Henry said, "You're saying this shark specifically hunts people?" He asked, dumbfounded.

John waved his hands. "Of course, that's what I'm saying. That's why it flips small boats and rafts like y'all's. It knows that it will get a reward. And it's sad to say, but if a body doesn't turn up, they will get labeled as having drowned, just like all the others."

Tim put up his hands. "How many people do you think this shark has killed?" He asked.

"Trust me, you don't want to ask him that. The old man's got this shark pegged for every missing boater for the last twenty years," boomed the voice of Captain Jake Taylor.

"I take it you don't believe that?" Cheryl replied.

"No way, I believe this thing is a real monster, don't get me wrong, this shark has killed a lot people, and if we don't stop it. This monster will kill a lot more. But, it's not responsible for every water related death out here like my father believes.

Besides, sharks are opportunists. Look, every attack so far has been on people in the water or fishing on small boats with bloody bait. As my father said, it's going after prey it thinks is weak. In this case, that happens to be people.

We aren't made to hunt in the water; we know it and the shark knows it." He turned and looked pointedly at his father. "I need you to steer us up into the bay, take her slow. The last thing we need is to run aground." He told him and then headed below deck. Henry assumed the other man was finally going to get some rest.

John snorted and made his way up to the control room so he could pilot the ship. Looking out at the other boat, which was almost completely submerged, he hoped they wouldn't share the same fate.

Together they kept shining their lights off the side of the ship, looking in vain for anything in the water, just in case. After a few more minutes of this, they gave up. The speed boat was now far behind them. Hopefully, the Coast Guard would be able to find more than they did and notify their next of kin.

Captain Taylor had said they sounded young, like a bunch of kids on a joy ride. God, Henry hoped he was wrong. Leaving the deck, he went down below trying to put all thoughts of the speedboat out of his mind.

....

Something was nagging Cheryl, but she couldn't quite put her finger on it. She had spent most of the time below deck reading or pretending to read. So much had happened and, to be honest, she wasn't sure how to process everything she was feeling. And the last thing she'd wanted was to have to talk about it.

The last few days had been a nightmare and now they'd basically been shanghaied and forced into helping with this insane shark hunt. Cheryl had been in the water. She knew all too well the fear of knowing that a predator was right behind you. She and Henry had been lucky, and she knew that. If they hadn't been, they never would have made it to the ship before the shark got them.

Yes, they'd been lucky, lucky that they swam faster than the others. She thought darkly.

And now they were going to hunt it? Kill it? How far were these men willing to go? She wondered.

Part of her had wanted to leave with Tyson. He had held it together on the raft and seemed like a good man. She knew that if she'd pressed the issue, Henry would have agreed to it. If this trip had shown her anything, it was that she still loved her husband, and while she trusted him, like her, he was way out of his depth. Even with a shark in the water, she felt like Tyson could have gotten them to shore.

Cheryl would have tried to convince Henry, not that it would take much, but she didn't like Aaron. Something about the man rubbed her the wrong way. Once she'd seen the raft staying on the ship, even if it meant hunting the shark hadn't seemed like a bad idea. Anything was better than getting back in the water when an honest to God man-eating shark was prowling around looking for prey.

Across the deck, she looked over at her husband. When she looked at Henry, she no longer just saw a middle-aged, over-worked man, who did nothing but work and come home before passing out on the couch.

Instead, he reminded her of the man she had first fallen in love with; a man who wasn't afraid to take action when the time called for it. She couldn't remember at what point he'd sunk into himself and lost his ambition. He had gotten to where he never wanted to leave the house for anything other than work. The only thing that had been more stagnant than his career had been their love life, which was another area she'd wished he'd taken more action in.

And I hated him for it, she thought guiltily. Not that the blame was all his. Things hadn't turned out how she'd thought they would after college, either. And in some of his failures, she saw her own and punished him for it.

Cheryl almost dropped her light when she realized what was bothering her. "Henry!" She yelled over to him.

"What's up?" He replied, looking up sharply from the water and crossing the deck over to her.

"What about Tyson and Aaron?"

Henry and Tim looked at each other, confused.

"What about them?" Henry asked.

"They are in a small raft trying to get to shore, right? Based on what John said, wouldn't that make them the ideal prey for this shark?" She asked.

Henry and Tim both cursed at the same time.

"I'll go tell John," Tim said, running towards the control room.

Henry turned off his light. "They are still several hours ahead of us. Maybe they have made it by now," Henry said, sounding as if he were trying to convince himself more than anyone else.

Cheryl shook her head. "I don't know, it's such a small raft and that little engine... if they aren't there by now, they've probably run out of gas. Or are at least close to it. You don't think they planned it this way, do you?" She asked conspiratorially, getting closer to him as she did, wrapping her arm around him and pulling him close so they could talk quietly together.

"What? Like letting them leave to use them as bait?" He asked incredulously.

She said nothing. Instead, she watched as Henry's face flushed. "I don't know. I mean, sure, it was crazy to let them leave, but they'd forced the issue and the Taylors didn't want to force them to stay. Not taking us to shore is one thing. Forcefully keeping us here is another all together in the eyes of the law. I'd hoped they'd done it to keep peace on the ship. Besides, Tyson is a seaman, and he seemed confident about his ability to get that raft to the shore."

He rambled lamely. Cheryl knew he was trying to convince himself more than he was trying to convince her.

"You don't sound sure." She was all she said, taking a step back and leaning against the rail. Any other time being in the water at night with the wind in her hair would be a cause for celebration. Now it only filled her with dread.

He sighed. "Because I'm not. I don't know. All I know is that I won't let anything happen to you. You and I are going to be okay. We're going to get through this."

"Promise?"

He pulled her into a hug. "Promise." He whispered as the ship once again changed course.

Chapter 15

The night was calm as they made their way slowly across the bay. Tyson held the throttle down as far as it would go. The little engine pushed the raft as fast as it could. It just wouldn't be fast enough. Cursing himself inwardly, he knew that there wasn't anyone to blame for their situation but himself. Sure, he'd let Aaron goad him into it, but Tyson should have known better than to set out in this little craft. He knew soon the engine would sputter and die, but at least they had solid land on either side of them.

All they had to do now was decide which shore they wanted to go to, Virginia or Maryland? If he'd taken the time to think things through, he would have waited until the Taylor's ship was closer to one or the other before taking the raft.

"Which way do you wanna go, Aaron? Keep in mind we don't have too much gas left." He asked, stopping what he was doing for a moment to look over at Aaron and wondering for the hundredth time how the hell he'd allowed himself to be talked into this. The other man had been absolutely no help the entire time. Tyson would have been better off if he'd done this on his own. A big part of him wondered if they shouldn't have just stayed on the ship with the others.

Maybe they would have been fine back on that fishing ship, but he hadn't felt like standing around on that deck while Captain Jake Taylor and his father chased around their own personal Moby Dick. From the moment they were rescued, he knew the reason those two were out here. They had that faraway look in their eyes of men obsessed.

This was why when Aaron had suggested asking for a lifeboat Tyson had given in so easily. Last thing he wanted was to get between two crazy fishermen and their catch.

Aaron sat there, his beady eyes glancing back and forth. "Which one's closer?"

Tyson snorted and decided they had passed by Cape Charles at least an hour ago. He was sure of that. He decided on Virginia and took a hard left, aiming for a bright bobbing and blinking buoy. If they were lucky, once they hit the shore, they should be close to Portsmouth or Newport News and could flag down a car.

He hoped that was true, knowing that his own geography skills were shaky at best.

But, he knew damn well he was guessing and grasping at straws at this point. There weren't enough lights on the coast out here for them to be around either of those two cities.

This had been a terrible idea. He was the first mate on the yacht, one that did pleasure cruises in the Atlantic, not some adventurous seafarer like he imagined himself to be when he was chatting up lonely travelers at the bar.

The way his luck was going, they were more likely to wash up in a state park than anywhere near an actual city, but at least it was the closest landmass for them to hit. Personally, as long as there was land at this point, he didn't care.

He just wanted to be out of the water.

The calmness of the water had helped them to make a great time, so perhaps his luck wasn't all bad. If it had been rough out, they would have been completely screwed. This little raft would have flipped or been blown off course hours ago.

Aaron cleared his throat. "I'm glad we didn't stay out there with them, even if we end up having to swim to shore." He said with an exasperated sigh.

Tyson looked over at him. "Why do you say that?"

"I saw that thing, man," Aaron replied, putting his head in his hands. "I was the last one pulled aboard and if I had been a little slower, it could have been me. I could have been that fish's dinner."

Tyson had been trying his best to forget about the shark. He had never seen anything like it before and he prayed he would never see anything like it ever again, but he knew it would swim in his nightmares for the rest of his life. For the first time, he was actually scared of the water.

"Me either." He told him. "In fact, I think I'm going to be looking for jobs onshore for a while when we get back."

"Have you been on a sinking boat before?" Aaron asked him as they closed in on the buoy.

Tyson laughed, "No, until this trip I had never been on or even seen a ship go down like that. Captain Patrick should have known better than to charge into that storm on a damn pleasure yacht. Especially one that wasn't in the best shape. He'd been putting off major repairs for years. That tight-ass bastard should have known better.

Of course, I'll play real dumb if any of ya'll try to sue his estate. His family shouldn't have to pay for his mistakes." He shook his head and realized that once they got out of the water, there were still going to be a lot of headaches ahead of them. People were dead, and the someone was going to have to carry the blame for that.

Aaron was no longer paying any attention to him.

"What is it?" He asked.

"It's nothing. I just thought I saw something in the water," Aaron replied, looking over the side of the raft out into the water.

"Probably nothing, maybe a carp. I think they jump. I'll be honest, I was never much of a fisherman." Tyson replied, glancing over to where Aaron was looking. "Yeah... see, man, there's nothing there."

They were now between the buoy and the shore, when the engine sputtered, just slightly letting them know that this was it. They were about to be completely out of gas. The shoreline was still a suitable distance away, worst-case scenario they'd paddle, but they were close enough that Tyson believed he could swim it if he had to.

He'd be exhausted by the end, but he'd make it. Aaron, on the other hand, might be in some real trouble if it came to that. He thought, looking at the other man's out of shape body.

Tyson was just happy to see the shore; all of Aaron's talk of seeing stuff in the water was starting to spook him. He didn't want to think about anything swimming around them right now.

The engine sputtered one more time and then finally died.

"Shit," Tyson groaned.

"What's wrong?" Aaron asked, his voice cracking halfway through. Tyson swore that even under normal circumstances, Aaron would still have jumped at every little sound and shadow. Aaron was a walking bundle of nerves and the sooner he was on land and away from him, the happier Tyson would be.

They were now floating aimlessly with the current drifting farther from the shore and back towards the buoy. Looking around the raft, he realized a little too late that they didn't have paddles or anything that could be used as one.

"We're going to have to swim," Tyson said resigned. The last thing that he wanted to do was jump into the water at night.

Not again.

"Maybe you can swim and I'll sit here and you can go get help," Aaron said, nodding happily at the idea.

Tyson sighed, "Look even if we are somewhere close enough for that to happen, by the time I got back with help, you would probably be halfway out the bay and back into the ocean with no way to steer yourself, and no way to contact anyone."

Aaron was about to say something else when the choice was taken from him. Something hit the small raft hard and fast, tipping it on the side and throwing both men out into the water.

Tyson gasped for air as he clawed his way back to the surface.

Not again! Please, not again, he thought as he struggled back to the surface. Gasping as he broke free from the water.

He didn't waste any time though and swam as hard as he could towards the buoy; the shore was too far away, and he knew he would never make it in time. He threw everything he could into it. A lifetime of working and living around the water was finally paying off as he deftly crossed the short distance.

He heard Aaron behind him, splashing in the water and panicking. Aaron, on the other hand, wasn't a strong swimmer.

"Help me!" He shouted,

But Tyson couldn't stop, to stop meant death. When their boat had flipped, he knew without a doubt that something had rammed them from underneath.

Just like last time.

Aaron didn't realize it yet, but they'd just dropped a rung in the food chain, and right now it was every man for himself.

Tyson felt something swim by him in the water and he kicked out as he neared the buoy. He kicked again and this time his foot connected with something solid and he felt something big swim away from him. Wasting no time, he clamored up the side of the buoy as fast as he could.

Why did it swim away? Tyson wondered and then he remembered the nose.

You were supposed to hit a shark in the nose. How'd he forgotten that? It was one of the first things he'd learned in his dive class. However, back then, he couldn't imagine being that close to a shark, let alone punching it.

"Aaron hit it in the nose!" He yelled out to the other man, who was still splashing around wildly, but somehow slowly getting closer to the buoy.

Tyson leaned over the edge with his arm outstretched, only to yank it back as a fin breached the surface behind Aaron when he reached out for Tyson's hand. The look in his eyes was one of confusion as Tyson pulled back in fear. It was the last look the man would ever make.

When Aaron felt the pressure and searing pain, he knew it was already too late. He didn't even have time to cry out as he was dragged into the water.

Tyson could only watch as the other man was pulled down into the water after a brief and useless struggle. He then pulled himself further onto the buoy, grasping onto it for dear life.

He knew it was still down there circling and waiting for him to make a mistake and wind up back in the water. Eyes wide open, he clutched tighter onto the rails. One thing was for sure: it was going to be a long night. Tyson thought miserably.

Chapter 16

They continued to throw chum off the side of the ship as they made their way up the bay, all of them vigilantly looking for any signs of the raft. So far no sharks had made an appearance and the only things coming up to take the chum were large skates which glided alongside the ship.

"Damn," John muttered for the thousandth time, and took another swig from his hip flask; which was the only sound to break the silence while they all worked.

"Hey, Henry, we're getting low," Tim shouted over to him.

Henry ran across the deck and dumped out another bucket of freshly chopped chum. Wondering just how much of this stuff they had aboard. He was up to elbows in fish blood, guts and offal. If he wasn't so worried about Tyson and Aaron's safety, he would have taken a shower and gone to bed by now.

For two hours they had searched to no avail, instead deciding once again to chum the waters and draglines. John had convinced them they could do both. Hit two birds with one stone was how he explained it. Though Henry had serious doubts, he couldn't shake the feeling that Cheryl was right and in the end, the shark was more important to them than saving Tyson and Aaron.

With those dark thoughts in his head, he went back to work chopping up chum. What had started out as frozen fish was now thawed out and ripe. Flies buzzed around the dead, rotting fish, but Henry couldn't even smell it anymore as he hacked them up.

His sole focus was to chop up as much as possible, hoping if they ran out of chum, they'd go to shore. Even though he didn't truly believe they would, it gave him something to do. What's more, it gave him something to hope for.

There was no way they would turn back; poor Tim was getting just as obsessed as the Taylors. Henry watched as the other man baited the large hooks and fervently ran up and down the deck, checking the lines.

The water all around the ship was bloody. Lit by the overhead lights, it looked like they were dragging a dark crimson cloud with them up the bay. Between that, the smell of the fish he butchered, and the churning of the waves, Henry had almost lost the contents of his stomach more than a few times.

Even the deck was stained a dingy red. That was also on old John he'd gone below and emerged with a cooler, to help strengthen the chum. Right away, Henry should have known he would not like whatever the other man pulled out.

And he didn't. It was pig blood and guts. Which they mixed in a bucket with fish parts. It all stank terribly and now it coated the deck where they'd spilled it more than a few times, trying to puncture the bags. He didn't even want to think about how much of it was on him. Henry couldn't wait to get home and throw these clothes away for good.

Henry hoped it wasn't an omen for things to come. He kept telling himself that as soon as they got the shark, they'd be home free, but even he doubted that was true.

"This is disgusting," Cheryl said, handing him a rag to clean up as she came over to him.

Henry tried his best, but it did little to get most of the gore off of him. His hands still had a reddish tinge, and Cheryl even found a stringy bit of fish in his hair. "I know... but once we're out, they'll have to stop and resupply, right? And then we're all off the boat and they can go fishing for a man-eater by themselves for as long as they want." He told her.

She looked across the deck to where Tim and John were still working. "You sure about that?" She asked him,

He wasn't. It was late, yet none of them had stopped. Not to rest, not to eat. Hell, he hadn't even seen one of them take a piss in the last three hours.

"Why pig parts anyway?" Cheryl asked him at the same time that John came over to grab another bucket.

"That's easy," John replied. "It's the closest you can get to people."

A cruel sneer had accompanied that last bit. A sight that was becoming more and more common on the old man's face. The closer they had gotten, the less he had talked. Ever since the other two had left, he'd seemed to get meaner and more driven.

It was as if the old man could taste his prey in the salt air. That energy seemed to take hold of Tim as well. He followed the old man around the deck like a trained hunting dog waiting for its next command.

"What's gotten into you?" Henry had asked him when he first noticed his strange behavior.

With a faraway look in his eye, Tim had replied. "I want to see that shark die, Henry. I can't stop thinking about it. I need to see it die to make up for all those people I brought out here for it to feed on."

After that, they hadn't spoken. Tim, like John, was battling his own demons, as well as fishing for the beast, which left Henry on the deck trying to keep up.

It was madness.

Simple madness. Even Jake, the captain, seemed to have caught it. He was silent as a ghost in the control room. Henry could almost feel his gaze staring out into the water as if by some strange power the captain could see into the depths and leer at the shark.

The Angry Lady was the name of the ship, thought Henry. He almost laughed. It was an apt name since almost everyone on it seemed fueled by hate.

That's the feeling, he realized.

Righteous anger. That's what gripped Tim and the others as they plowed ahead, no matter what the cost. He wondered if they actually wanted to save Tyson and Aaron, or if they just hoped the two had attracted the shark.

Either way, now he and Cheryl were being pulled along for the ride.

A hard pull on one of the lines caught them all off guard. Tim ran across the deck to the taut line. Henry and Cheryl stood where they were watching grimly, and hoping that their misadventure would finally end.

"Fish on!" Yelled John as he ran over and cranked the line in.

Tim helped him and slowly the heavy rope-like line on the wench came up. Whatever was on the other end fighting against them the whole time, Henry didn't know if he wanted to see what was on the other end of it or not.

It was a shark, all right, but it wasn't their shark. No way, this one was much smaller. Too small to be the vicious man-eater that Henry and the others had seen devour people in front of them. John spat in disgust as he looked at it wiggling around the deck. Tim held the shark down while the old man deftly removed the hook.

Henry watched the whole spectacle, shocked at how much nerve both the men showed. Even a small bull shark was big enough to take someone's hand off, especially if that hand was groping around its mouth for a hook.

When they tossed it back in, the shark swam lazily, splashing around. "It's just getting its senses back," John told them.

But as they all watched off the side of the deck, something else happened. With the spotlight pointed at the water where they'd just released the shark, the waters splashed violently and turned red. John ran to grab something from below deck while the others watched.

"What's happening?" Tim asked, watching in shock as the shark floated up to the top of the water, obviously dead. Something had ripped chunks out of it and bitten almost in two.

Henry had a nagging suspicion, but didn't want to voice it. He had watched a documentary on sharks and knew that they would readily feast upon their own kind, especially one that was showing signs of distress.

"Bigger shark!" Shouted John in obvious glee as he ran back to the side, holding aloft what Henry could only call an honest-to-God harpoon in his right hand.

They attached it to a coil of rope that he tossed to Tim to tie off. Poor Tim stood there in shock as John reared back his harpoon and threw it with all his might. His timing was perfect. Just as he threw, the much bigger shark had resurfaced to devour more of the smaller one.

The harpoon flew through the air and planted itself in the shark's side. With the harpoon deeply ensnared in its side, the shark wasted no time and dove beneath the water.

That won't kill it, though, thought Henry. That would be too easy.

Too late did they all realize that Tim had not tied off the rope. The coiled rope snapped tight around him as the big shark used its powerful muscles to dive further down. Tim screamed as the rope dragged him to the side of the ship, his legs going off the side.

John and Henry both ran forward to grab him. They tried to hold on as best they could.

"Cut the rope, damn you!" Henry yelled at John. The old man did nothing, making a point of not looking at Tim's face at all as he strained in pain. Tim did his best to hold on to the side. His veins stood out from the effort, and the skin around the rope was red and raw. Instead of tying it off, he had coiled it around himself. They needed to cut it, but John wasn't going to do it and Cheryl seemed frozen where she stood.

John stared out at the water as if he could see down into the depths and see his prey. Henry grabbed for John's knife to cut the rope, but John pushed him away. As soon as Henry stumbled back, both John and Tim went right off the side of the ship.

A loud splash followed them. Henry ran to the control room. In less than a blink, both men had gone overboard. He didn't feel like he had time to use the intercom system, not that he'd know what button to press anyway. Jake looked up at him as he barged in.

"Drop anchor!" Henry told him, panting for air. "Tim and John just got pulled overboard!" He shouted as loudly as he could.

Jake looked at him incredulously. He had dark bags under his eyes and it took him a moment to move, but Henry didn't have time for explanations and ran back down to the deck. He quickly put the rope ladder in place. Looking around, he grabbed one of the lifesavers and tied it off to a rope. Both men had already surfaced.

"Did you see it?!" John yelled as he trod water. "Go get a gun!"

Cheryl was leaning over the side. "He's crazy Henry. He's really crazy. I think he wanted to go over the side!"

Henry could only shake his head unbelievingly; the old man was more worried about killing the shark than saving his own life, or the life of anyone else for that matter.

Eat your heart out, Captain Ahab, Henry thought with distaste as he threw the ring in closer to Tim, who was also treading water, but was now pale as a ghost. They needed to get them out now before it was too late.

Tim groped for the little float lamely, finally finding the ring. He grabbed onto John, even though the old man fought him tooth and nail to get away so that he could fight the shark. The Angry Lady's anchors found purchase and the ship ground to a sudden stop. The whole time, Henry and Cheryl pulled both men closer and closer towards the rope ladder.

Behind them, he saw something he couldn't believe: a harpoon handle stuck up out of the water about the same time as a dorsal fin rose in front of it. Now there was no mistaking what exactly was swimming towards the two men.

Henry pulled harder; they were almost there. Jake ran down from the control room and helped.

He watched as the rope ladder pulled taut as John put his feet on it and began the climb up the side of the ship. Tim was right behind him. Henry pulled the lifesaver up and threw it on the deck, hoping they wouldn't have to use it again soon. Then he ran to the ladder and helped haul John back aboard.

He went back over to the side after Tim, who was shaking with fright and trying to make his way up the ladder at the same time. Henry reached out for him and they locked hands. He could only watch as the shark, now halfway out of the water, launched itself at Tim like an airborne torpedo.

Tim screamed in pain and fear as the shark latched on to his right leg, severing it at the knee as it dropped back down into the water. Tim fell from the ladder, but Henry still had his hand. Henry tried to hold on, but Tim's hand was wet and slid from his grasp. Henry could only watch as his friend dropped into the water.

Tim screamed as he resurfaced, his stump bleeding profusely, reminding Henry of the buckets of chum they had been dumping along with the ship most of the day. He threw the lifesaver back overboard.

"Grab it!" He called over the side, shining the spotlight on the water.

He watched as the shark circled Tim, as if savoring the meal to come. Anytime Tim moved to grab at the life preserver, the shark would come in between them, forcing Tim to swim back.

"Jesus," Henry muttered. He felt like he was going to pass out or be sick. Or both.

"Oh my God." Cheryl had muttered and then turned away from the scene. They both stood silently at the side, his hand in hers, feeling helpless as he watched the shark play with its food. Henry knew he was about to watch his best friend die and there was nothing he could do about it.

John suddenly re-emerged, rifle in hand, and fired wildly into the water.

"Watch out for Tim!" Jake shouted at him.

If John heard, he made no sign; instead, he kept firing, the water around Tim and the shark. Jake rushed at John and they grappled for the rifle.

"Put it down before you kill the man, you old idiot!" Jake shouted as he pried the firearm from his father's hands.

John snapped out of whatever had possessed him. He opened his mouth to say something, but a scream cut him off. The shark had apparently tired of its game. The water was now a deep red, the shark's tail cutting the water back and forth as it tore into Tim. Its football-shaped head twisted every which way as it pulled him apart. Even after Tim had stopped screaming, the shark continued butchering him until there was nothing left on the surface.

Afterward, it dove back down into the water. Leaving those aboard The Angry Lady to watch in silence as the lone harpoon handle sank below the dark waters, which left no trace of Tim or the shark.

Chapter 17

Tim was gone and there was nothing they could do about it. Part of Henry wanted to take a swing at John right then and there, but he knew it wouldn't make him feel any better. And the bitter old man wasn't worth hurting his hand over.

Even the Captain was now staring forlornly over the side of the boat. None of them spoke. Henry wished he'd tried harder convincing Tim. All of them should have stayed below deck and let the Taylors carry on their hunt alone. But hadn't he wanted to see that shark die just as badly? Henry thought guiltily because, of course, he had. Just like the Taylors and just like Tim, he too had wanted to see that thing dead.

Instead, he lost his closest friend.

Henry had gotten sick over the side of the boat shortly after and tears still streaked down his face. Cheryl kept rubbing his back. Tim hadn't just been his friend after all. She'd known him for almost as long. Hell, he was the best man at their wedding.

"This madness has gone on long enough!" Jake yelled suddenly, breaking the silence.

"We're so close." John protested weakly.

"No, we're done...you hear me? No more dragging people into this. We should have taken these people to shore from the start. Now look, we've got two in the water God knows where and one in a shark's belly. These folks aren't fishermen dad, getting them involved in this shit was a bad idea and it ends here."

"But-" John began.

"No, go up top and take us to the nearest port. These people are going home," Jake said sternly.

John looked like he wanted to protest further, but let the rifle dangle by his side and grumbled as he marched past them up the stairs to the control room. Now that John was steering the ship, Jake stowed the gear spread out across the deck. There would be no more lines in the water or chum going overboard, not anymore.

Once everything was cleaned up, Henry went back to man one of the lights. Captain Taylor did the same, both coming to the same conclusion: that it wouldn't hurt to keep their eyes peeled for Aaron and Tyson on the way back. Cheryl, on the other hand, had gone back below deck.

Henry wanted to go with her but knew that if he wasn't busy doing something. Anything that he'd end up bawling like a baby over Tim's death and that wouldn't help anyone right now.

....

Jake didn't care at this point whether his father would understand his decision to abandon the hunt. His father had been acting like a madman ever since they'd gotten on the water. Sure, Jake wanted revenge, wanted to end the nightmares that had plagued him since he was a child, but his father needed it on a level that even Jake couldn't understand. Needed it like a man needed air and was willing to sacrifice anything and anyone to achieve that goal. Something which scared Jake more than the shark in the water.

His father had sulked the whole way up the stairs. And seeing him like that, Jake knew that without a doubt, he had done the right thing. With a tired sigh, he kept searching for Tyson and the others, knowing that his father could no longer be trusted out on the deck.

Old John kept The Angry Lady moving at an even pace, staying in the deeper water so that they didn't bottom out. That's the last thing they needed at this point. In the distance, they could see the twinkling green light of a buoy.

Henry saw it before him and called out. Jake quickly came over, and they looked around desperately for any sign of the others. But they didn't see any. The buoy, still a suitable distance away, was the only thing out there.

"Hey, keep your light steady!" Jake told Henry as he moved up beside him.

Henry complied. Jake felt bad yelling at the man like that, but sometimes that's what it took to keep people focused. Especially during an emergency, his time in the water had taught him that lesson. Besides, he thought he'd seen something moving in the water, but he wasn't sure. Or perhaps he was and simply hoped that he was wrong.

"I see it!" Captain Jake yelled in triumph, Henry's spotlight now angled off the starboard side of the ship.

Running over, Jake could just barely make out the handle of the harpoon as it breached up above the water. The shark was circling the ship, but now, thanks to the harpoon, they could get it.

Kudos to the old man. He had gotten that thing in there deep, Jake thought happily, and ran down below to fetch his father's rifle. He found it in no time and by the time he got back to Henry's side, he already had it loaded and ready to fire.

"Keep it steady," Jake told Henry again as he shouldered his father's rifle and Henry did his best to keep the light on the shark.

"Do you have it?!" The intercom blared as John's booming voice echoed across the deck.

In reply, Jake aimed and fired. The gunshot echoed out over the water and caused his ears to ring. Water exploded up near the harpoon handle and it disappeared from sight.

"Did you get it?!" The intercom blared again.

Jake and Henry stood looking over the rails, the spotlight illuminating the water for any sign of the shark.

They saw nothing.

Jake went to put the rifle back on his shoulder, deciding it might be a good idea to put another bullet in the same place, just in case. Henry kept the spotlight moving around, scanning the water.

Suddenly, they heard screaming from the other side of the ship. Both men took a second to look at one another before running towards the sound. All thoughts of the shark were forgotten.

Standing at the front of the ship, they could now clearly see the buoy. And there in the blinking green was a figure standing up and clinging to the buoy as it bounced in the bay's current. A figure that was screaming at the top of their lungs to get Jake and Henry's attention.

It had to be Tyson or Aaron, Jake hoped, unable to make out who was doing the screaming.

"Why did you stop sho-" The intercom blared before it cut off, replaced by a nasty grinding noise as the bottom of the ship hit a rocky sandbar.

Jake grabbed Henry, and the rail just as the worst of the shaking began. He knew what had happened, even if he didn't want to believe it. His father, so eager to get the shark, had stopped paying attention to the depth finders up in the control room, and the ship had paid the price.

Jake swore if they were lucky, they'd be able to make it to the other side. If they were really lucky, they wouldn't be taking on water when they did.

Still clutching the rails, both men were thrown forward as the ship listed hard to one side. As it did, they both slid down to the lower side. Before he could grab hold of the other man, Henry was thrown hard on the rails and went over. Jake grabbed him just before he went overboard, only to go over with him. Jake had one hand on the rail and the other on Henry, unable to pull himself up and unable to let go. They hung there tentatively as the ship finished cresting the sand bar.

It entered the deeper water with a groan still listing to one side. Jake swore again as smoke rose in the back of the ship. And when it didn't right itself, he knew what was happening. The Angry Lady was sinking. His pride and joy was now taking on water, and there was absolutely nothing he could do about it. And the worst part was deep down inside, he knew that all of this was his fault.

He looked down at Henry, who met his eyes and nodded. Then, taking a deep breath, Captain Jake Taylor let go of the rail.

Chapter 18

Henry panicked as soon as he hit the water. He was all too aware of what was waiting for them down there. He pumped his legs as hard as he could, pushing himself up from the water and up back up into the night air. Desperately he tried to reach out for anything around to grab onto, but only found open water all around him.

For a moment, he forgot what it was he was doing as he saw the ship. The Angry Lady didn't look good. She was listing to a side and even from where he was, he could tell it was taking on water a lot of water. Soon, it would suffer the same fate as the yacht it had rescued them from.

Cheryl! His mind screamed.

His wife was still on the ship, and it was going down. And there's still a shark in the water, he reminded himself and swam faster, remembering just how dangerous the beast was. Last thing he wanted was to share Tim's fate. He swam purposely, praying that the shark was far away from them.

Even he wasn't optimistic enough to think that any of Jake's shots had hit home. And even if they had, he wasn't sure that anything could stop that shark.

Swimming to the listing side of the ship, he grabbed onto the side rails and pull himself over the side. Water was rising on the deck and pouring down the stairwell that led below. The ship groaned and rolled harder onto its side. Henry scrambled to hold on and, as it slowed, he made his way to the stairs.

He groped around the entrance of the stairway, finding it hard to navigate while the ship sank slowly down on its side.

With his hands and arms fully outstretched, he pushed himself down into the darkness of the belly of the ship.

"Cheryl!" He called out again, praying for an answer.

He waited several seconds for a reply as more and more water rushed past him. Already he could make out a significant amount of flooding in the kitchen area, at least what he could see in the flickering lights.

"Cheryl!" He cried out again. "Where are you?"

He splashed through the kitchen, feeling like he was in a funhouse the way all the bolted-in furniture angled from the walls. The water was now up to his waist, with more pouring in. Out of the corner of his eye, he saw a red bag. It had a little cross on it.

When they had gotten aboard the yacht, he remembered Tyson's safety brief. He had shown them all a bag like this and what it contained: emergency supplies, bandages, water bottles, and a flare gun.

Yes, Henry thought, that could come in handy.

He had little time to spare, and he needed to find Cheryl now and get to the buoy before the shark realized they were in the water. He grabbed one of the life jackets and put it around his neck. If she was injured, Cheryl might not be able to swim by herself. God knows he hoped she wasn't hurt.

"Please, please be okay," He kept muttering to himself.

The sound of someone coughing came from down the hall. Cheryl.

He moved as fast as he could, sloshing through the water with every step. In the back, there was a small bathroom. The door had water pouring in and as he got closer, he could hear someone pounding on it. Cheryl was there, looking around wildly, coughing, and sputtering through the crack in the door as the water continued to pour in. There was a cut on her head, and she looked at him wildly, fear and panic spread across her face. They both knew that if she didn't get out of there, then she was going to drown.

"What's happening?" She asked him, still coughing up salt water.

"We're sinking." He replied, moving to her, and knelt on the other side of the door. As she pushed from below, he pulled, straining against the weight of the water, which was now up to his stomach. Even working together, they couldn't get it all the way open. A small sliver of a crack opened up. Henry felt the water flood past him and he pulled more. The opening was just wide enough and straining, Cheryl was able to slide out and into his arms.

In that moment, there was so much he wanted to say to her, but all he could do was stare. Taking in every inch of her. Happy beyond words that she was once again safe in his arms.

"We need to get out of here." She told him, looking around at the devastation and cutting off his train of thought.

Henry didn't want to let her go, but knew that she was right. They didn't have time to waste.

Quickly, he took the life jacket from around his neck and put it over hers. Then he worked on the clamps, making sure that they would support her. Cheryl put a hand to the back of her head, and it came away bloody. Unlike the cut in the front, the gash in the back of her head would probably need stitches. Which meant there was absolutely nothing they could do about it now.

Damn. As soon as they got into the deeper water, the shark would know. He'd watched enough shark week to know that Cheryl's blood would be like ringing a dinner bell for that thing.

"Alright, listen to me. I know there's a lot to process right now, but you have to keep your head above the water at all costs. And, if by some miracle we make it out of here, don't fall asleep, you might have a concussion too." He told her, trying to remember every bit of emergency medical knowledge he'd learned in scouts. Now he wished he'd paid better attention back then.

She nodded and carefully they navigated their way back up to the deck, Henry leading from the front and pulling Cheryl along behind him. It was hard going with them walking on the slick walls as the water continued to rise and debris floated around them.

They made it back to the kitchen area when Henry saw his problem. Getting down without stairs hadn't been too hard, but how were they supposed to get back up?

"Wait!" Cheryl yelled, pulling him back as he made his way to try his luck.

"I'm going to get up there and once I'm up, I'll reach back down and pull you up." He told her.

Although he doubted his plan would work, they didn't have a better plan. What they really needed right now was some rope.

"No," Cheryl said. "That's John's room." She told him, pointing to one of the bunk rooms.

He caught on right away and headed over to it. Luckily the door was open, and it was on the other side he could climb in by pulling himself up. He found what he was looking for immediately; hanging from a bandolier on the now horizontal bunk was a shotgun.

Pulling it out, he saw it had four shells attached to its side. It had been a very long time since he had fired a gun, but he knew that if he was close enough to use it on the shark, four shots was being optimistic. He would be lucky to get one off before he became a floating Happy Meal.

He dropped back down to where Cheryl was standing and saw that the water had risen more; now it was up to his chest. At least it made it easier for them to get out. Getting Cheryl to hold the gun in one hand and grasp on to him with the other, he swam up the stairway as far as he could. Without prompting, Cheryl locked her legs around his back and Henry grasped the rail on the side of the stairs with one hand and pushed off the bare wall with the other.

His outreached hand found a perch: the doorway, and he pulled them up with all his might. As they made it into open water, the ship lurched, the bow plunging downwards, and the control room rose into the air. Soon the entire doorway and below deck area was lost beneath the water. Henry could make out figures in the control room: the only people it could be was Captain Jake and his father.

They'd made it.

A loud boom filled the night, and the ship shook violently as the engines blew up. First, all Henry could see was the billowing black smoke, but then he saw the flames that followed it. No time to worry about that now. He knew he had to get out of the water. He just hoped the others had a plan.

In the distance, he saw a harpoon handle rise from the water. He didn't need any more motivation after that.

"Hang on!" He shouted to Cheryl as she clung to him.

That was all the prompting he needed. Using the ship's dry side railing like a ladder, Henry slowly made his way to the control room that now hung in the air overlooking it's quickly sinking bow.

He climbed harder; knowing that below them, circling the sinking ship, was a very pissed and hungry shark.

Chapter 19

When Jake fell off the side, he'd been prepared. He took a nice deep breath before he hit the water. Kicking out as soon as his head went under, Jake could push himself up and break the surface, taking another long steadying breath as he took stock of the situation.

He heard Henry splash into the water. For a moment, he wondered if he'd need to go save the other man, but then watched as Henry broke the surface. The other man swam towards the partially submerged deck.

The captain didn't have time to fret about Henry; he didn't even have time to worry about his ship, which was quickly sinking. All he could do was wish Henry and Cheryl the best and make his way towards his father.

He would not lose any more family members to the shark. Not as long as he was still alive to say anything about it.

Climbing onto the deck, he carefully made his way to the staircase that would take him up top. Jake hung tightly to the staircase as he climbed it like a ladder. One wrong move and he'd have a shortfall back down to the deck. One that was sure to break something before he slid into the water.

Underneath him, *The Angry Lady* creaked and moaned as she took on more water.

"I know, old girl." He mumbled, feeling tears come to his eyes as he apologized to the ship that had served him so well over the years.

For the first time, Jake understood why some captains went down with their ships. He shook the dark thoughts out of his head as he climbed closer and closer towards the control room door. Straining, he pulled himself closer to the control room.

He gripped the side of the doorway. The door now swung freely with the rocking of the ship. Hanging over the water, Jake pulled himself into the control room. Hitting the shoal had thrown his father against the controls, which was probably the only thing that had kept him from being thrown out of the doorway.

"Dad?" Jake called and got no response.

From the way everything was hanging off the walls, he would have to climb to his father, who had enough sense to strap himself into the chair before they wrecked.

Damned, foolish old man. Jake swore.

But looking at his father hanging limply in the chair, his anger wouldn't even stir. All he could feel was pity.

Jake pulled himself the rest of the way inside and dragged himself against the wall on the right. He nestled against it as he tried to come up with a plan to get his father. Something hit him in the head as he crawled against the wall. Reaching up, he found that the radio was swinging around on its cord, freed from the small clip that kept it close to the captain's chair.

Holding it, he could just barely hear the static that let him know it still worked, albeit faintly. Now all he needed was to know their last position. Then he could call it in shark or no shark. A soft moan came from the chair. His father was stirring.

"Dad, are you okay?" Jake asked him.

John Taylor opened eyes, and for the first time in Jake's memory, the man looked old. Old and tired. He watched as John tugged on the belt and looked around. Understanding came into his eyes as his gaze finally rested on the open doorway.

"Shit," He muttered.

"You're telling me," Jake replied. "Look, can you see the GPS?"

John looked around and found it. "Yeah, it's flickering."

"Okay, what are the coordinates?" Jake asked him.

John read them off to him, squinting as the screen flicked back and forth. Jake said them out loud to himself so that he would remember them. Then he called it in, hoping that someone would pick up their transmission. After the fifth call out, someone finally did: a Coast Guard station.

Thank God, Jake thought to himself. He quickly rattled off their location and situation.

Afterward, he let go of the radio. Now they could deal with his father's situation. How the hell were they going to get him down without injuring him, or worse, falling into the water below? There was no way that the shark had swum off. They weren't that lucky, especially not lately.

His father swore. "Dammit, I think we have another problem," John told him, disgust clear in his voice.

"What is it now?" Jake asked hesitantly, wishing that for once something would go right on this damn venture.

John Tyler twisted around in the seat that had become his prison. The straps clung tight, restricting his movement.

"The buckle won't undo." He cursed again. "The damn thing is busted and I ain't got anything to cut these straps with."

It was Jake's turn to swear.

Still crammed off into the corner of the wall, he dug through his pockets until his fingers finally found his small pocketknife. He would have to climb up there somehow and cut his father down. All he had to figure out was how to do it in a way that wouldn't send his father falling like a rock out the door into the water below. Glancing at that water, he realized that whatever he was going to do, he would have to do it now, because the water outside the doorway was getting closer.

Jake hoped Henry had found his wife and made it out all right. If the water was this high in the control room already, then the decks below had to be completely submerged by now.

No time to dwell on that, he thought, shaking himself.

He climbed slowly towards his father.

"Hang on to the bottom of the seat." He said as he pulled his way closer. Finally, he grabbed down at the base of the chair. It was awkward and hard to hold, but it gave him just enough stability.

That pole made a scraping sound as he did. The captain's chair wasn't designed to support that much weight. With one arm hanging on and the other swung above him, sawing away at the straps, Jake's foot slipped, and he found himself hanging directly above the open doorway. Pulling himself up, he was able to get his feet back under him, but barely.

If his father fell, then it would be both of them taking the plunge.

"Jake. Stop." His father boomed suddenly.

Jake stopped mid-saw, shocked at the outburst. "We don't have time for a talk right now."

John Taylor made a disgusted sound. "No, dammit, boy, look, my legs busted. When you cut me down, don't stay behind for me. Y'all just get to the buoy. Okay?"

"Dad, what are you going to do?" Jake asked, not understanding what he was hearing.

"Doesn't matter. Just agree." John replied evenly, his voice carrying the same stubbornness it had when Jake was a boy.

"Okay, but we are going to be fine, dad. The Coast Guard will find us. Just don't do anything crazy," Jake replied and went back to sawing at the strap with the knife. Wondering if he believed any of the words he just said.

He finally cut through. His father dropped and now they both clung desperately to the captain's chair. The metal pole screeched, and the chair sagged some, but it held. Two figures were suddenly in the doorway, clinging to it for dear life.

Jake couldn't believe his eyes: it was Henry and Cheryl.

Henry's eyes were as wide as a saucer. "The shark's circling below us."

The words hammered into Jake's mind as the chair squealed once more; the metal was starting to give.

Chapter 20

The ship rocked again before settling. Now it was sinking fully. Soon the whole thing would be completely underwater. If they were going to make a move, they had to do it now.

Cheryl and Henry clung to each other and the side of the wall. Both doing their best to stay out of the open doorway. No one wanted to get in the water until they had to. Henry thought, but they'd have to, eventually. The look on Jake's face told him the same thing. The older man was grim and drawn as he slid down from where he was hanging onto the captain's chair to where Henry and Cheryl perched against the wall.

"We are going to have to jump," Henry said as Jake joined them.

Jake nodded and then motioned at what was hungover Henry's shoulder. Remembering the shotgun, Henry slid the strap of his arm and handed it to Jake. He figured the captain could put it to better use than he could. Besides, he still had the flare gun if he needed to scare the shark off.

"I know, but when we go, it has to be all at once," Jake replied after he finished looking the gun over. "It's the only way any of us will have a chance."

"A chance at what? Getting eaten?" Cheryl retorted angrily.

"Girl's not wrong," John told them. "Look, I'm not going to make it swimming there. Hell, my legs are give out as it is. The least I can do is buy you all some time."

The others looked at him. Henry and Cheryl said nothing.

Henry watched as different emotions played out on the captain's face. Grief, anger, acceptance. Finally, he spoke up.

"No, John, that's crazy," Henry said, even though he was more or less in agreement with the old man. He didn't like it, the idea of leaving someone behind, but he reminded himself that Cheryl and he wouldn't even be in this mess if it weren't for John.

And Tim would still be alive.

Jake still hadn't said anything. They watched as he just kept staring at his father and shaking his head.

The ship rocked violently, and the water on the other side of the doorway started getting closer.

Jake gave his father an awkward hug. Henry thought it was clear that neither man was used to showing that kind of affection, but at least it seemed the captain had come to a decision.

John and Jake looked at each other, neither one of them seeming to trust giving a voice to what they were feeling. They nodded to each other one more time and Jake, Henry, and Cheryl went out the open doorway.

Instead of jumping, they amended the plan. Again, using the stairway like a ladder, they climbed down into the water. Most of it was now underwater, so they didn't have far to go. The bow of the ship was still visible. It was a decent swim, but they could ride it down without having to worry about drowning. The only thing they had to worry about was the shark.

The cold, dark water eagerly greeted them. Henry swam as fast as he could towards the other end of the ship. Henry knew there was no time for subtlety. The water on either side of him splashed with the sounds of Jake and Cheryl doing the same thing. There was no doubt in his mind that the shark still circled the slowly sinking ship.

He just hoped it hadn't spotted them yet.

The flare gun was safe in a box and tucked into his lower back, his belt keeping it in place. Once they skirted the bow, they could then fire the flare from the top. It was their best bet to get some help.

That was, of course, if there was anyone around to see it. Henry thought miserably.

The bow was closer now. The only way on it would be to climb the rungs up the side, and Henry couldn't help but view them as some sort of hellish monkey bars.

Henry got to it first and climbed, pulling himself out of the water and upwards along the side of The Angry Lady, for what he hoped would be the last time. It was hard going hanging vertically and propelling oneself forward, especially while trying to clutch the box with the flare gun to his lower back.

If that fell, then they were screwed.

Henry's first sign of trouble was Cheryl's cry. "Captain Taylor" She shouted, "Hurry!"

Looking back as far as he could, Henry still couldn't tell what was going on. He had no choice but to continue upwards.

The captain, on the other hand, was scrambling to get out of the water. He had pushed Cheryl up ahead of himself and was now having a time getting up. The bars were wet and so were his hands. No matter what he tried to do, he couldn't seem to get a good perch.

His hands were slipping and sliding, and he couldn't stop thinking about his father all alone in the control room waiting to die.

When Cheryl screamed his name, he knew he was in real trouble. From the terror he heard in her voice, he didn't even have to wonder about the cause of her distress. He turned in the water and saw it: a harpoon cresting the water. The weapon was still firmly lodged in the beast it was supposed to kill. Now it looked almost like a second dorsal fin as it sped towards him like a hungry torpedo.

Jake tried to pull himself up again and slipped again back into the water.

Calm deep breaths, he reminded himself, doing his best to fight off the panic that he felt brewing. He was a seafaring professional, and he would not die like this. That thought slowly became a mantra as the shark barreled through the water towards him.

Putting one hand in front of the other, he pulled with all his might, which wasn't much at this point, but this time, he got a handhold. He pulled himself just far enough up that he could slip a leg through one rung. Using that leg, he pushed up and caught another and was now climbing it like a ladder, if you climbed them upside down.

He took a glance at the shark below, which had circled under them: a death sentence for anyone who slipped and fell.

He climbed higher, taking his time as best he could and gripping tight at the rungs when the ship shook. It wouldn't matter if they got to the top of this damn thing or not. By the time anyone responded to the flare, this ship would be beneath the water and they would be shark food.

He felt his panic returning. The same panic he'd had as a child when the shark took his brother and circled the buoy, waiting for him to fall in. Now he was in that same position. And the shark knew it had all the time in the world.

At the top, Cheryl and Henry waited for him; they were looking at something in the distance. Jake sat beside them, completely out of breath, and turned to look. A buoy was out there bobbing, maybe less than half a mile. A suitable distance to swim, but from the looks on everyone's faces, he knew they were thinking the same thing as he was: that buoy could be their only hope.

It wouldn't be comfortable, but at least it wouldn't sink.

"I think we should try for it," Jake said, breaking their silence.

It was awkward sitting up there, trying to stay balanced on top of the sinking ship. Another rock and the hull groaned as the water they had just escaped barely escaped from crept closer at an alarming rate. The decision was being made for them.

Something large splashed down in the water behind them. It came from the direction of the now soon-to-be submerged control room. They all knew what it had to have been or, more aptly put, who.

"He's bought us time. It's now or never," Cheryl said.

The others nodded in agreement.

"Trade me," Jake said to Henry, pointing at the flare gun box he still carried.

"Sure," Henry was happy to lighten his load. He didn't really know how to use the thing, anyway.

"Now or never, you two," Jake told them.

Cheryl and Henry jumped and began swimming as hard as they could towards the buoy. Normally Jake would have told someone swimming even a small distance like that to be careful not to over-exert themselves, but in this case, drowning would be the least of their worries.

He opened the flare gun box and loaded the gun. It had over six shots in the box. When he'd bought it for the ship, he never thought he'd actually have to use it. From way up on his perch overlooking the other half of his sinking ship, Captain Jake Taylor of The Angry Lady kept his eyes peeled for the man-eating shark swimming below him.

Then, holding the flare gun above his head, he pulled the trigger and lit up the night.

Chapter 21

John Taylor felt more tired than he had ever felt in his entire life. He was so used to being full of anger or rage when he saw the water, but now, as he looked down at the waves, he only felt relief.

It was all finally ending. The fight that he'd dreamed about for so long was finally here. With one more steadying breath, he took the plunge out the door.

Gripping the shotgun tight to his chest, he hit the water and immediately kicked up, pushing himself up above the water so he could see the threat when it came. Because one way or another, the shark would come for him.

John just hoped his son would understand. There were so many things left unsaid between them. If only there had been more time, but he knew it wouldn't have done either of them any good. At the end of the day, the Taylor men were just too stubborn.

Jake had turned out a lot like him, no matter how much they'd tried to raise him to be otherwise. John smiled at the thought of his son, so much like himself, he knew that he'd understand why it had to end like this.

Swimming through the water, his busted leg was causing him more trouble than he'd thought it would. Mentally, he tried to push past the pain as he made his way to what was left of The Angry Lady's once-proud deck. Most of it was completely underwater now, but there was enough left that he could at least stand upright.

It was the only way he was going to have a chance to send this shark on a one-way ticket to Hell.

John didn't try to swim silently. In fact, he did the opposite, splashing loudly and making as much sound as possible. He wanted to get its attention. If he couldn't stop it here and now, then he could at least buy the others some time while they tried to get to safety.

His fingers brushed against the deck of the almost fully submerged vessel. He did his best to keep his back to it and pushed himself up with his legs groaning in pain, sprained, not broken. He still had some movement, but he could feel them going numb. Taking the safety off, he racked a shell into place.

Raising the shotgun, he aimed it at the shark. The shark was a dark grey torpedo shooting towards him. He fired as it crashed into him. A chunk of its side blew out, but the beast didn't waver. The recoil from the shotgun pushed him backward and made him lose his already precarious footing.

"Fuck you!" John screamed in the water as the shark smashed into him. He roared in pain as its jagged, saw-like teeth sank into his thigh. Ripping and tearing as the beast tried to take his leg off.

His hand trembled a little as he pulled the knife from his pocket. From both age and fear, John didn't need to be a doctor to know he was dying.

It was an old folding knife, but it would work fine for what he wanted it for.

"I hope it hurts, you son of a bitch!" John yelled, grabbing the shark by the harpoon to pull himself higher up. He gazed into the shark's lone, dead black eye and shoved the knife in as far as he could.

He was already dizzy from the pain and blood loss and as the shark shook him again; he dropped the knife before he could stab it again. John tried to twist the harpoon handle doing anything in his power to hurt the shark, but the world was fading as his weak, trembling hands fell off the harpoon handle, and the shark dove down, taking John Taylor with him.

Chapter 22

As Henry plunged into the water off the bow of the once proud ship, all he could feel was an overwhelming sense of dread. His heart pounded in his chest and felt like it was about to jump right out of his skin. Breaking the surface, he started swimming towards the buoy. Cheryl was ahead of him; she'd hit the water first and had immediately started swimming.

The water was rough and fought against them as they made their way. Already Henry was feeling the adrenaline he'd had earlier fade. Cheryl had slowed down, too. Both of them struggling against the current. He just hoped it was getting closer, and it wasn't just his imagination.

The buoy was an unwavering beacon of light in the distance. A distance they may have somewhat misjudged before jumping overboard, but now they had no other choice but to stay the course.

"Don't slow down and whatever you don't stop!" Cheryl shouted back at him as she continued to push forward. Just then, a gunshot echoed out across the water.

It had come from behind them. They both slowed for a moment, listening, but there wasn't a follow-up. Henry didn't want to think about what that meant, so with grim determination and newfound fear he continued towards the buoy.

Was Jake in the water?

He hadn't heard another splash. Maybe the captain had gone down with his ship after all. Or maybe something got him before he had the chance to get away? Henry didn't like that thought, not one bit, especially the flicker of hope that came with it. The guilty, shameful hope that the deaths of the Taylors would buy Cheryl and him enough time to escape.

The buoy was close now. Close enough that they'd soon be able to climb up, but Henry was downright exhausted and if he wasn't careful, the current would start pulling him away. From the sounds of Cheryl's ragged breathing, she was feeling the same way.

These last few days had put both their bodies through the wringer and neither of them had been in that great of shape in the first place. Sure, they fit in slim clothes, but that didn't mean they could swim miles in a single go.

They were now side by side, almost pulling each other along. As they got closer, they could see someone on top of the buoy, shouting and jumping and waving to them, "Over here! Come on guys, you're almost there."

Henry wanted to shout back, but if he stopped now, he didn't know whether he'd be able to swim again.

They could hear the man on the buoy yelling. "Hurry! Get out of the water!" Jumping up, the figure on the buoy pointed out towards the water.

Henry's heart started hammering again, reminding him what he'd been so afraid of in the first place.

"It's coming!" The man shouted again.

Those words sent a surge of adrenaline running through Henry's body. He felt his breathing quicken, and he tried not to panic. Panicking now would only get him killed. The buoy was right in front of them, so he refused to look back. He felt like if he did, it would be the last thing he ever did.

As they neared the buoy, hands came down. The figure standing on it helped them. Henry pushed Cheryl ahead of him, making sure that she was the first aboard. He boosted her up and the person on the buoy quickly pulled her over the side.

Henry was next and for a minute, he didn't think he was going to make it over. His feet kept sliding on the side of the buoy and he was worried that his attempt to get up would pull the other man in. The man yanked hard. It felt like Henry's arms might pop out of their sockets, but the next thing he knew, he was lying on the floating buoy beside his wife.

"Looks like none of us succeeded then." The man said solemnly.

Henry sat up, hugging himself to the cramped platform beside Cheryl. The voice sounded familiar. And as his vision cleared, he got a good look at the other man and instantly recognized him.

"Tyson?" Henry asked, not quite believing his eyes.

Tyson sighed, "Yeah." Looking just as shocked as they were.

Cheryl sat up, staring at him. "But how?"

Tyson shook his head and spat, his gaze looking out over the water to the now retreating fin and harpoon handle.

"How do you think?" He asked them bitterly.

A silent pall settled over them as they absorbed his words.

"What about Captain Jake?" Cheryl asked them.

They all looked back toward what was left of the ship.

"He made his choice," Henry said. "Now we can only hope that he survives it."

"He's got the flare gun though, and he's no doubt a stronger swimmer than us three," Henry said, thinking about it.

Cheryl groaned. "Do you really think a flare gun is doing him any good in the water?"

Tyson sighed. "She's right. Hell, he's just as likely to shoot himself by accident as he is to hit the shark if it comes up under him."

Henry felt the last of his hope for Jake Taylor's survival leave him. He had hoped the captain would make it. Ever since they had pulled them from the water, he'd thought of the other man as some unstoppable force. Until he'd seen him lose again and again to that damn fish. Henry started laughing then, all the adrenaline fleeing from him as he succumbed to his mirthless hysterics.

The others stared at him. "What's so funny?" Cheryl asked.

"It's a fish." Henry sputtered. "A big, goddamn fish. And the fucking thing has us swimming and screaming all over the ocean, a fucking fish. Nothing more." He finished staring at them, finally calming himself down.

Tyson spat out into the water again. " You're right, nothing but a big scary-ass fish. I tell you one thing; I'm going to be eating a lot more seafood in the future. Just to be petty." The bigger man said with a laugh.

Cheryl just shook her head. "I'm going to get my ass into the gym swimming laps. I didn't realize how out of shape I've gotten until this. I used to be one hell of a good swimmer."

Henry just laughed. "Darling, you can go to the gym all you want, but I'm not going into anything deeper than a bathtub for the rest of my life." He replied, making them all laugh so hard the buoy rocked and swayed. Out in the distance came a thunderous roar.

"Oh, great, the last thing we need is a damn storm," Henry muttered.

"No." Tyson said. "That's not thunder. Sounds like ole' Captain Taylor is putting that gun to use."

They all looked out over the waves, straining to make out any figures in the growing darkness. They all jumped as another roar split the night, followed by silence.

Cheryl was the first one of them to break the silence. "Do you think he got it?" She asked no one in particular.

Tyson cleared his throat. "I hope so, God, I hope so."

All three of them stood there, looking out over the dark water, wondering whom they would see in the darkness: the victorious Captain Jake Taylor or the shark; battered, bloody, and still hungry. As they all stared in silence, a sudden noise broke their reverie. The unmistakable sound of splashing was getting closer. It looked like they would have their answers soon enough.

Chapter 23

Jake knew the moment that his father died. To him, it felt almost like a physical blow. Even though most of his life he'd despised the man, part of him still couldn't believe he was gone.

When the gun went off, only once he knew. His father, had he been alive, would have kept shooting the shark until the shotgun jammed or ran out of ammo. He was a hateful, vengeful man and had gone out the way he'd lived.

Looking over the side he was about to jump off, Jake paused. He'd been about to jump and swim to the buoy, but he wasn't ready yet. Whether it was the duty to his ship or anger over the death of his father, he wasn't sure. Right now, he was too numb, and it was all much too raw.

Opening the flare gun bag, he quickly cracked open the little orange pistol and jammed one flare into its barrel before closing it. He knew that unlike the shotgun, it wouldn't kill the shark, but it would hurt it.

Maybe even blind it enough, so it left them alone for good. Then, wounded and blind, some other shark would come along and eat it. Which was a small bit of karmic justice Jake could live with even if he wouldn't present to see it happen.

When he laid eyes on the shark, his breath caught in his throat. This time it wasn't just from the fear of being on the quickly sinking ship and knowing that eventually he was going to wind up in the water. No, it was because of the direction the shark was coming from.

The harpoon handle, at least what was left of it, stuck out of the water coming from the direction of the buoy. Jake swore loudly. The damn thing had cut off his escape. Trapping him on the ship until he had no choice to get in the water.

He couldn't out swim a shark. Even a wounded one could do laps around him in the water.

Did Henry and Cheryl make it? He couldn't help but wonder. He hadn't heard any screams. God, he hoped they did. He prayed he wasn't the only one left. If he were, there was a very good chance that the story of what happened here would die with him.

He didn't want to think that way, but even Jake knew that no matter how long he'd been on the water, nothing had prepared him to face a shark in its own element.

How could one shark do all this? He thought and wondered for the first time if they weren't hunting for some sort of monster after all. And just like Ahab, they'd lost everything in the pursuit.

And like Ahab, it wasn't just on the whale. He and his father had brought this down upon everyone. In their need for revenge, they'd let their arrogance drive them to ruin. Too late to wallow in pity now, he watched as the harpoon got closer, forcing him to make a decision.

He could barely make out the large dark body gliding through the water, getting closer to where he waited. Soon he'd have to make his move, and he'd only get one chance to make this work.

One chance to live.

Jake wrapped his legs around the top of the rails and straddled the sides. He aimed the flare gun and cocked the hammer back; he almost pulled the trigger by accident as his wet boots slipped on the slick metal rails. Almost throwing him off into the water.

Saving himself in the nick of time, he restudied his aim.

The harpoon got closer. The shark seemed to swim differently. Slower... that was it. Apparently, his father had hit it after all, good for him. He hoped it would be enough.

He felt sweat drip down his face. His nerves were beyond frayed at the thought of failing this one job: of failing to finally end the existence of the creature that had haunted his dreams since he was twelve. The same creature that had torn his brother to pieces in front of him.

The harpoon was now within shoot distance, with the shark circling near where Jake was perched as though it knew he was up there. Bile rose into his throat as he realized in horror that the shark wasn't circling, waiting for him. It was looking for leftover pieces of his father. All this death and the shark wanted more.

He felt his finger tense on the trigger, but it was still too far away, and it would be foolish to waste a shot. No matter how badly he wanted to take it.

Steady. Steady now, he thought as it came closer and closer, slowly weaving around the top of the water.

The shark headed towards him and as it slowly came to the surface; he fired the flare gun. With a hiss and pop, the flare shot across the knight a glowing arc of phosphorescent flame that slammed into the side of the shark. He watched in wonder as the great beast thrashed and splashed before diving into the water. The flare burned out with an angry hiss.

"Take that, you son of a bitch!" He laughed, quoting one of his favorite movies. He doubted that something like that would be enough to kill it, but he knew it had hurt it and hurt it bad. That was enough for him. It would have to be. He was less than five feet from the water now. If he stuck around any longer, he was going to wind up as fish food.

Jake shoved the flare gun back into the bag and pulled out his knife. Clutching the blade tightly between his teeth, he jumped from the railing. It was a quick drop and before he knew it; he was in the cold water below.

As soon as he hit, Jake started swimming, pushing as hard as he could through the water towards the buoy. Dragging the bag behind him in the water.

He glanced backward occasionally as he fought against the tide. Part of him was terrified of what he might see rise behind him. The other part of him hoped for it. He wanted to look the damn thing in the eye when he sent it to hell.

It was that kind of thinking that got us all in this mess in the first place; he thought bitterly and pushed on. He was getting tired. Jake hadn't swum like this in a long time. But the buoy was getting closer. If he just kept it up a little longer then he'd be there. And then he'd be safe.

At least for a little while, if this trip had taught him anything, it was that safety was never guaranteed.

There was a loud splash behind him, and he almost stopped swimming. Behind him he could almost see the harpoon handle as it started heading in his direction. The shark swam up near the surface of the water, clearly confident that he couldn't get away.

The buoy was now insight. Even though the shark was still making its way lazily in his direction. Squinting through saltwater encrusted eyes, he could make out people standing on the buoy. If he didn't know better, he'd have said they were cheering him on.

The undertow pulled at him, but he kept kicking harder and faster. He hoped that the shark had given up, but even he knew he wasn't that lucky. Jake was just surprised that he'd gotten this far with a shark in the water after him.

That thing was too hateful to die, he decided as he neared the buoy. It shocked him to see the people on it waiting for him. Apparently, the others had made a clean escape after all. Especially Tyson, who deftly pulled him up over the side. Questions that would have to wait as Cheryl pointed behind them and screamed.

Chapter 24

When Henry saw what she was pointing out, he cried out too, unable to stop seeing as the large fin rose behind Jake. But they couldn't do anything about it as the shark rammed the buoy and Jake rolled off the end and back into the water.

For a second Cheryl teetered and Henry lunged forward to grab her, losing his footing he slid forward catching her and almost sending them both over the side.

His face against the cold, wet, metal buoy, he watched the shark lazily swim through the water and pulled his wife tighter against him. Why was it moving so slowly he wondered?

Had they actually injured it or was it playing possum? He didn't care how slow it was swimming, nothing could convince him to dive into the water and find out. Henry wasn't a hero. Not in that way. He just hoped that Captain Taylor was smart enough to get out in time.

He watched it as it rounded the buoy again. Could it not see them?

If it was injured, why wouldn't it leave them alone? A dark thought shot through his mind. Maybe it wanted to take as many of them with it that it could before it died. He shuddered just thinking about it.

Tyson's hand was outstretched, and the man was pleading with Jake to take it. But, he didn't Henry watched in horror as Jake turned away and put his back up against the buoy facing the shark. Henry wanted to think that perhaps he figured the shark was waiting for him to turn his back and attack him while he was being pulled up. But, he doubted it. He couldn't help but figure that Jake saw his opportunity for revenge and took it.

Henry could only watch as the harpoon rose and was then followed by a fin. The fin got closer and closer as the shark headed straight towards Captain Taylor.

In the water, Jake could feel those dead black eyes on him as he slowly paddled backward pressing his back up against the buoy. He'd already tossed the flare gun up over the side. They'd have a chance he'd made sure of it.

Doing his best not to splash or struggle too much in the water; the last thing he wanted was to give that thing a clear line to strike. He wanted it to investigate slowly. That way he'd have plenty of time to find the perfect place to strike.

In the glaring, green light of the buoy, he could clearly make out the mess his father had made of the creature's right eye. He could also see the pepper marks that spattered its thick skin and the burns following that. The beasts' flesh was in tatters and looked like something out of a horror movie. He couldn't believe that it was still alive.

Well, at least he had hit it. Much good that did him. Blood leaked out of the wounds. As it swam closer to him, Cheryl, Henry, and Tyson all clamored towards the side of the buoy. They shouted and smacked the sides, anything to turn its attention to them.

But they didn't realize that Captain Jake Taylor was exactly where he wanted to be.

The shark was heading in his direction, and he brandished the dive knife in its direction. He only had one chance at this. He just hoped that he'd live long enough to take it. As far as plans went, it was a shitty one, and if he told the others, they would have tried to pull him out against his will.

If he was honest, he wouldn't have blamed them. Part of him even wanted to let them, but this had to be finished. It was the only way that it was ever going to stop.

And he was going to stop it here and now, he swore mentally.

It headed straight towards them. Without warning, it sped up. The shark's lazy swim erupts into a thrashing as it shot through the water like a torpedo. He braced himself as he watched rows and rows of jagged teeth rise out of the water, heading straight towards him.

Everyone on the buoy screamed. Jake may have too. But he wasn't sure all the air was forced out of his lungs as the shark crashed into him. Its teeth ripping into his stomach as he brought his arms around and jabbed the knife as hard as he could into the shark's remaining eye.

Its head dove, tearing into him as he hung onto the knife, not giving into its attempt to throw him off. Blackness crept into the edges of his vision as he fought to hang on. He was too close now.

His thumb found the button on the side and pressed it down. The compressed air stored inside shot out and there was a little pop, followed by a meaty explosion of gore as parts of the shark's head blew apart.

Suddenly, the tension against him seemed to ease as the shark stopped pressing itself into him. The jaws of the great beast were still locked on him, not that he minded anymore. Jake couldn't feel it, anyway. The darkness now crowded his vision. With his hand still on the knife, Captain Jake Taylor drifted off to eternal sleep.

"Oh my God!" Cheryl exclaimed from the buoy as Henry, Tyson, and her watched Jake and the shark now entwined with each other in death slowly sink into the water. Fading out of sight from the eerie, flashing green light.

Henry watched in horror, wondering why the other man had chosen such an end. Before realizing that maybe this was the only way it ever could have ended.

The shark never would have stopped and even if he had left this time, a man like Captain Jake Taylor never would have been able to live with himself knowing that the shark was still out there.

On the buoy, he clutched his wife while Tyson kept an almost silent vigil looking out over the water. He'd already fired off a couple of flares. Soon they'd be rescued and put it all behind them.

"They'll reappear soon," Tyson told them.

Henry didn't need to ask who he was talking about.

"But, I hope they don't. He would have liked a water burial, I think. Maybe it's best if they don't." Tyson said again, almost to himself.

"What do you mean?" Cheryl asked him.

Tyson shrugged. "No one is going to believe a shark is responsible for all of this. Even if they find the remains."

Henry nodded. Maybe they wouldn't. But he decided he didn't care if anyone believed them. He'd tell the truth as he knew it. The two Captain Taylors deserved that much and so did the victims of the shark.

He leaned against the buoys tower and pulled his wife close. He closed his eyes, feeling her warmth and taking comfort in it as he heard the unmistakable sound of helicopter engines in the distance. With a sigh, Henry closed his eyes, content with the knowledge that they'd survived their vacation and that they wouldn't have to take another for a long time. Even as he closed his eyes, he could hear the steady thumping of helicopter blades as their would be rescuers got closer.

About the Author

J acob Peyton, is an introverted shut-in trapped in a cave surrounded by books somewhere in rural Virginia. When he's not reading or writing, Jacob is probably either wandering the Mohave Wasteland in Fallout New Vegas or is somewhere in Tamriel on ESO. Or watching the 1980 Flash Gordan and laughing maniacally around 24-45 minutes in when Flash gets beat down by a bunch of guys in tights. (Sorry Flash, but seriously if you haven't seen that do yourself a favor and check it out.) On the rare occasions that Jacob is pried from his cave, he enjoys hiking, traveling, and climbing around in attics and bookstores after old pulp paperbacks. If you wish to hurry him along in writing the next book, compliment or yell at him.

Feel free to shoot a message at authorjacobpeyton@gmail.com Please no spam, unless it's cool spam. (But even then please don't.)

You can also follow him at Twitter: @jkylepeyton

or on Facebook: https://www.facebook.com/authorjacobpeyton

But, for best results, mosey on over to www.jacobpeyton.com[1] and make sure to sign up for his

---

1.   http://www.jacobpeyton.com

newsletter, which is chock full of some rather cool stuff.

Also, if you found yourself enjoying this book "Even if only a little, please take the time to leave a review anywhere you like. (But, if you need suggestions, Goodreads is always appreciated.) Because even shut-ins like me need to keep their caves properly provisioned.